Janice B Scott

Poisoned By Yew

And Other Stories

Janice B. Scott

Beasant Books

DEDICATION

For the Famous Five
and Timmy, the dog(s)

CONTENTS

ALSO BY JANICE B. SCOTT

The Polly Hewitt series of novels:
Heaven Spent
Babes And Sucklings
Vengeance Lies In Wait

Short Story Collections:
Children's Stories From The Village Shepherd Vol. 1
Children's Stories From The Village Shepherd Vol. 2

ACKNOWLEDGMENTS

My thanks are due to my family, particularly my son Alex, for persuading me to publish this collection, and to all the family for their continued encouragement (amidst many rude comments and much laughter.)

1 FOREWORD

I wrote this motley collection of twenty four short stories over a number of years. They are indeed motley. Some are very short and can be read during a five minute coffee break. Others are longer, but can be read in bed in that short space of time between wakefulness and sleep. The whole book is ideal for train or plane journeys. All the stories are light-hearted, and several are tongue-in-cheek. Some have been published previously in other anthologies.

Some stories are humorous, and indeed, most have an element of humour within them. Several of them reflect my background of the church, but perhaps in an unexpected way.

I have grouped many of the stories in a way which seemed logical at the time. Thus there is a group of five stories featuring the same characters (the group which begins with *'Deadly Keys'* and contains *'Poisoned By Yew'* the title story of this book), a group of slightly bizarre or futuristic tales (beginning with *'Halloween Experience'*) and a couple of gentler, 'heart-warming' (as our American cousins might say) stories. These latter have a stronger religious element than some of the others, and *'The Smallest Angel'* is a Christmas story suitable for children as well as adults. All the other stories are adult stories, but none contains what has become known in the media as 'adult content'. Although several of the stories are murder mysteries, they are all gentle in character. None have chain saw massacres or anything remotely resembling gore.

The opening stories are very short, and each has a surprising ending. I wrote them for a bit of fun, so I hope you enjoy them in the same spirit.

I wrote some of the stories for competitions (and occasionally won!) but others just because I wanted to write them. While very few of them are overtly religious, some do contain a Christian message and none of them deny my own religious convictions. Although there are some nasty characters who act in unchristian ways, I would be unable to write anything which directly clashed with my own raison d'être.

The majority of these tales are written in the first person, but none are autobiographical. Honestly. Writing these stories has given me a great deal of pleasure. My wish is that you will derive equal pleasure through reading them.

Janice B. Scott www.janice-scott.com

2 A CRY FOR HELP

It happened last night. I was on the way to the train station to pick up Florence. Her train was due in at eleven o'clock and she'd been travelling for twelve hours, three of those hours spent waiting at Liverpool Street since she could only afford the cheapest ticket. That's daughters for you.

I was waiting at the traffic lights to turn right into the station when this car drew up alongside. I happened to glance to my left just as the traffic lights in the middle lane changed to green. As the car sped off, I saw a woman in the back seat mouth "Help!" at me.

For a moment I was too stunned to move—and I was stuck in the right hand lane. I had no option but to drive into the station, but as soon as I realised Florence hadn't arrived yet, I shot out of the other side of the station in hot pursuit of that car.

It wasn't long before I caught sight of the Daimler two or three cars ahead of me. Difficult to miss a Daimler, even for me who knows nothing about cars. Besides, there wasn't much traffic at that time of night. I tailed the Daimler through the back streets of Norwich, weaving in and out of parked cars, sliding down side roads, nipping through narrow alleys, even trundling down a cobbled road at one point. I thought we were going on forever, but at last the Daimler parked outside a three-storey, Victorian villa in a road of three-storey Victorian villas.

I wasn't so stupid as to approach. Hah! You thought I was going to charge in and confront them, didn't you? Not a bit of it, I'm not daft. I held back, but watched as the man—six foot four and big with it—hustled the woman—petite and blonde under the sodium lighting—up the steps and in through the front door. He had his arm around her shoulders, clutching her so tight she had no possibility of escape.

I made careful note of the name of the road and the number of the house, then rang the police. Some dolt of a police constable seemed to have

3

difficulty understanding me.

"Is that two Ts or one?"

Whoever heard of Scott—the surname—spelt with one T? Then the spelling of my address was interminable. It's not easy spelling Crescent in phonetic police-speak when you only know Tango, Echo, Romeo, and Juliet.

At last I was able to make my way back to the train station. At least, I attempted to make my way back to the station, but having never darkened this area of Norwich before, got hopelessly lost. Needless to say, I had no map with me, nor any GPS system. It took me ages, twisting and turning, looping and circling, until I managed to get back.

Florence was less than impressed. She looked like thunder. She turned her face away as I reached to kiss her, and she slung her multiple bags onto the back seat without a word. When I explained what had happened, she shrugged and rolled her eyes as though I was a complete idiot.

Huh! I thought. I just might have saved somebody's life, so what's a few minutes wait compared with that? OK, three quarters of an hour's wait, even.

The police turned up next morning. They showed me a photo of a petite blonde lady and asked if I knew her.

I studied it carefully and handed it back. "No. I've never seen her before last night."

"That's odd, Madam, because she knows you."

"What?"

"Apparently you met at a dinner dance three weeks ago."

Oh Lordy! That was when it all came flooding back. A slightly drunken event, the round table where we all had such a riotous time, that lovely couple who were so full of fun.

But I wasn't giving up yet. "Why did she ask for help, then?"

He smiled. It was a pitying, mocking smile. "You don't lip read well, do you? What she actually said was not *Help*, but *Hello*."

Florence was less than impressed. She shrugged and rolled her eyes.

3 A NO-NO

I spotted him the moment I stood in the doorway and scanned the room. The large red carnation in his buttonhole may have given me a clue. My eyes travelled upwards towards his face and I gave an involuntary gasp. What was a guy like that – tall, brown crinkly hair, gorgeous deep brown eyes, craggy features, slender build – doing in a hotel bar for a blind date?

I'm pretty sure he noticed my amazement, for one eyebrow lifted in a quirky sort of way and a slow grin spread across his face. Playing it cool, I sashayed across the room and slid onto the barstool next to him.

I held out my hand. "Jane Doe."

At that, both eyebrows quirked upwards and he laughed. He enveloped my hand in his large warm one and a tremor shot up my arm. "Abe Foreman at your service," he said with a slight, old-fashioned bow. "A glass of white wine for the lady?"

I laughed. He was nice. "Perfect," I said, and I wasn't only talking about the wine.

"Have we met before? Perhaps in my undertaking business, Jane Doe? In a churchyard, or something?"

"Ooh, macabre! Meet many ghosts?"

"Only beautiful ones," he purred, his eyes raking my figure, "in slinky red dresses."

What a smoothie! But I lapped it up. I'd been in two minds about the dress, not sure I wanted to resemble the special K girl too closely. Not that there was much chance of that, with her five foot ten, ridiculously slender figure. I'm only five five, and several pounds heavier. And no, I'm not revealing how many pounds. Still, his compliment was very welcome.

I've always maintained blind dates are a no-no, but this was the best blind date ever. I'd only accepted Sandy's suggestion when she agreed to a free week in June in her cottage in Corfu. I've been on Sandy's blind dates before, and without exception they have been disasters. Naturally I'd come armed with a pepper spray and my favourite penknife – OK, the blade is only two inches long, but it's terrifyingly shiny – just to be on the safe side. And I'd insisted on driving myself, for a quick getaway.

But now, with Able Abe Foreman, all was forgiven. Until, that is, the door opened and Sandy and Trevor stood there, together with a short, balding, paunchy guy. And when a leggy blonde appeared from the direction of the ladies and made a beeline straight for Abe, I realised my embarrassing mistake.

I blame my impatient gene, the one that gets me to parties half an hour before everyone else, and has me waiting at airports at least three hours before the plane is due to leave. I inherited it from my father, who was never happy unless he had the whole family marshalled and ready to go at least two hours too early.

My face flamed. Able Abe must have thought me such a fool. I mumbled my excuses and escaped, sliding off the bar stool and reluctantly joining Sandy and Trevor and Porky – whoever he was – and making sure my back was turned towards Abe Foreman and the leggy blonde.

True to form, Porky was a complete disaster from the moment he held out a moist palm for me to shake, and enunciated in a high, clear voice, "How do you do?"

I glared at Sandy, but she merely returned my look with a glance that said you're getting a cottage in Corfu for a week, what did you expect? I sighed, moved as far away from Porky as I decently could, and did my best to be relatively polite.

I breathed a huge sigh of relief when at last the band appeared. With any luck they would be loud enough to drown out any hope of conversation, and I would have the perfect excuse to turn my back on Porky in order to watch the dancing.

Ignoring Sandy's pointed glances which said dance with him or you're dead, I settled back in my chair, but bolted upright again when Abe Foreman sauntered past, brushing my arm as he led Leggy Blonde towards the dance floor. As an electric shock shot up my arm, I was so tempted to stick out a foot and trip up Leggy Blonde, but I had no need, for just at that moment she somehow collided with our table, sent all our drinks crashing over Porky, and landed with her head in his lap.

I don't know which was funnier, Porky's bulging eyes and panting breath as he took in Leggy Blonde, or Sandy's outraged expression, daring me to laugh.

Leggy Blonde disappeared very quickly towards the ladies, with Porky trailing hopefully but benightedly in her wake. Now was my chance to grab Abe Foreman and dance the night away, but I was foiled in my attempt.

My sister glared at me accusingly as though it was all my fault, snatched up Trevor and her handbag and said in tones that brooked no disagreement, "Come on, we're going."

Since Abe Foreman had wandered away out of sight, presumably to wait for Leggy Blonde to reappear, I shrugged and cut my losses. At least I could look forward to a week in the sun.

I stretched out on the lounger, lapping up the heat.

"This is the life," I murmured, as Caroline's long legs reappeared into my line of vision. She set down the tray of drinks, flicked her long blonde hair back over her shoulders, and settled onto the other lounger.

"It's all right for you," she grumbled, "but that was my best dress. And I had the devil's own job getting rid of that appalling guy."

"I paid for your dress to be thoroughly cleaned, didn't I? And you had a much better chance of getting rid of Porky than I did. After all, it wasn't you who was set up with him. By the way, where did you find Abe Foreman?"

Caroline gave me a piercing glance, and began to laugh. "Don't tell me you fancied him! He spent weeks trying to find a Jane Doe in the telephone directory. He searched the Internet, and kept going back to that hotel just in case you were there. Jane Doe! Couldn't you think of anything more original?"

I said stiffly, "As it happens, Jane Doe was entirely appropriate since Abe Foreman was an undertaker."

At that, Caroline doubled up. "Well, at least he has a sense of humour. Abe Foreman! He's as bad as you. And an undertaker! You really believed him? You have got it bad! Pity you told me not to reveal any details about you, on pain of death. Come on, drink up, we'll have a swim, then we'll wander down to that taverna in the village, the one I was telling you about."

I did as she suggested; there wasn't much point in arguing. Besides, we had nothing better to do.

It was a lovely little taverna. We sat outside under the trailing vine, at a rustic table. I hardly noticed the waiter, until he placed a large red carnation in front of me and murmured, "Jane Doe, I believe?"

If she hadn't been my best friend, I might have throttled Caroline, but I was too busy, wrapped in Able Abe Foreman's strong arms and exploring his luscious mouth. And was he ever able! Wow!

Who was it said that blind dates are a no-no?

7

4 THE TOWER

He forced his weary body onwards and upwards, ever upwards, hampered at every turn by the sack he dragged behind him, bumping it from step to step. He was so tired he no longer cared about the contents of the sack, if ever he had cared.

The steps seemed never ending. Ancient stone, crumbling at the edges, narrow and winding, dangerous. No wonder nobody ventured up here.

His breath was coming now in short gasps. He rested for a moment, wishing he'd thought to count the steps as he started. How many was it now? A hundred? Two hundred? Six hundred? He had no idea.

The sack was growing heavier with every step he took. He hefted it towards him, but there was no room on the step for both him and the sack so he had to rest it on the step below. This spiral stone staircase was medieval, leading him to the very top of the church, the tip of the tower, several hundred feet from the ground. It should be high enough, he thought, for his purposes.

The steps opened out into the ringing chamber where the bells were hung, allowing him a brief respite, but he daren't stop for long. He had to make it. Taking another deep breath he pushed on, hampered now by the wind swaying the tower. Was this normal, this terrifying swaying motion, this movement of the tower? Or would it collapse and him with it, never mind the huge sack?

He was stupid to have agreed to this, to have attempted it in one go. Someone else should be doing it, not him. He was too old for this sort of stress. But still he pressed on, ever upwards.

And then the spiral steps ended, suddenly, abruptly, without any warning.

He found himself straddling the bare wooden beams of the roof, his heart in his mouth as he stared down, down, down, between the beams. There was no floor. Suppose he slipped? It would be the end of him. He lifted his eyes. It made him feel weird, looking down. Was this vertigo, then?

He saw the ladder, clearly the final stage, but what a stage. Just an ordinary wooden ladder, propped carelessly against the wall and leading to a trapdoor in the roof.

His heart was thudding now, thumping painfully against his ribs. He wanted to close his eyes, but afraid of the gaps between the beams, dared not. Carefully, painstakingly, he inched forward, towards the ladder.

One hand closed on the rungs, the other dragged the sack. He wasn't sure how he was going to manage, the sack was so heavy now. He offered up a prayer, then forced himself to climb. When he reached the top of the ladder he was slick with sweat. He wedged his knees as best he could, and wound the arm carrying the sack around the ladder. Then he pushed on the trapdoor with his free hand.

It felt solid to his trembling limbs, but he heaved with all his might. It gave just a little, forcing him to climb another rung to gain the advantage. Then, with a final mighty shove, it was open.

He pulled himself through the narrow entrance, emerging into the wind as it tore at his clothes, but he was able to lower the sack onto the roof. He advanced towards the parapet, and for a moment was stunned at the view. He could see for miles over the countryside.

Then he looked down. They were all there. Anxious faces gazing up at him. He had half a mind to wave, but with a grim smile he opened the sack.

Taking out the first one, he threw it over the edge of the tower, impervious to the collective gasp which greeted his action. He went on tossing them over the edge until the sack was empty, not caring where they ended up. Then he threw the sack. No way was he going to carry that down again.

His job done, the Reverend Albert Hall slowly descended the steps.

That was it for another year. Another load of teddy bears had successfully abseiled - or near enough – the church tower at the annual church fete. Thank God.

5 ALARM

I heard it while I was walking to the 'Open Gardens' event.

You know the sort of thing. They happen all over the place these days, so that in the summer you can hardly set foot outside your front door without tripping over an 'Open Garden'. I usually avoid them like the plague because the cost runs way above the modest two pound entrance fee by the time you've bought a cup of tea and a slice of somebody's special chocolate cake, a couple of strips of raffle tickets, browsed the second-hand books and the bric-a-brac, and guessed the weight of the largest potato you've ever seen in your life. Then there's all the chat. Making small talk with random folk you happen to meet in somebody else's garden is not really my idea of fun. Not on a precious Sunday afternoon, anyway.

I decided to stroll along to this particular 'Open Garden' because it was within walking distance, less than a mile away, and for some obscure and inexplicable reason, I simply wanted to see the garden.

Of course, there were no other walkers. Everyone else had more sense. They all glanced at the sky, noted the black clouds overhead and got out the car. I, being a bear of very little brain, elected to walk despite the sky. I rather enjoy a solitary stroll along country lanes, although this particular solitary stroll was somewhat ruined for me.

It was as I walked along the lane that runs between the wheat field on the left and the hedgerow bordering the woods on the right, that I heard the car alarm. Only faint, but irritating none the less. There's nothing more designed to shatter your illusion of a rural idyll than someone's car alarm going off in the distance.

As I walked towards civilisation in the shape of the 'Open Garden', the shrill of the alarm grew louder. Clearly I was walking towards it. By now I was becoming intrigued. Why didn't someone turn the wretched thing off?

To my certain knowledge it had been going for at least ten minutes. As I turned down the street where the 'Open Garden' was situated (it was a corner property, a sure sign that the garden was opulently extensive) I realised that I would soon discover the cause of what was by now a clamorous screech.

Several houses before the corner, the noise was so loud and painful that I almost covered my ears. I stood for a moment outside the offending property, but no car was visible. I soon became aware that the car issuing the scream for attention was locked away in a garage. Even more intriguing. Were the owners away? Did the next door neighbours have a key? If so, why weren't they doing something?

Then an even more disturbing scenario occurred to me, probably as the result of too many crime dramas on television. What if someone was in the car with the garage doors closed, the engine running and a hosepipe stuffed through the window? I stood on tiptoe to see whether I could spot any exhaust clouds issuing forth from under the garage door, but I wasn't tall enough to see over the hedge.

I dithered, uncertain what to do. Should I bang at the front door and risk looking a complete idiot? Should I ring 999? Should I disturb the neighbours? In the end, I did what any concerned citizen would do. I kept my head down and continued on my way.

I reached the 'Open Garden', but the sound of that car alarm was still ringing in my ears – and in everybody else's I should think, since it was only a few houses away – but nobody else was paying it any attention whatsoever. I wandered round the garden, bought my statutory tea and cake and raffle tickets and what not, and chatted with the folks milling around.

I brought it up subtly. "That car alarm rather disturbs the peace, doesn't it?"

Everyone I spoke to had the same reaction. They all looked astonished.

"Hadn't noticed it," they said, with glance at me as though I was a little weird.

That was when the rain started to fall. Within seconds it was coming down in buckets, so we all trooped into the house, much to the politely hidden distress of our hostess. But with the garden effectively closed, people soon began to make their excuses and leave. I made a beeline for a couple who live in my street, and begged a lift home.

I thought no more about the car alarm until next evening, when I was watching the local news on television.

"A man was found dead in his garage yesterday evening," began the newscaster, with a suitably sombre expression.

My heart plummeted. This was my fault! If only I'd followed my instincts and rung the emergency services or called a neighbour, perhaps we would have been in time. How could I ever forgive myself?

Actually, I forgave myself in about ten seconds when I realised the story wasn't in our village at all.

And the car alarm? I later found out it was caused by the family cat being shut in the garage while the family went out for the day, so no harm done to anyone. Except perhaps, the cat.

The moral of this story? Since they are universally ignored, car alarms are a complete waste of time.

Alarming, isn't it?

6 DEADLY KEYS

"Got another stiff for you—from that church."

Jack had a grin the size of Norfolk. I clenched my fists in my efforts to maintain a poker face, but he just laughed. "Thought that would surprise you, Detective Chief Inspector! Never say I don't give you anything."

"I'm not entirely sure a second dead body counts as a gift, even for a homicide detective. But thank you for your kind thought, Dr. Death. I'll be sure to reciprocate—probably in kind, so watch your back."

At that he laughed even louder, and despite myself, I couldn't help grinning.

"Bet I solve it before you do," he scoffed.

"You're on. Fifty says I get there first."

"Last of the big spenders, DCI? If you promise to spend it on something black and lacy, I might even let you win."

I threw a spare kidney dish at him, which he caught with one hand. Not only the best pathologist in the business, he was also a former county cricketer, a fact he rarely allowed me to forget. I tossed my head and strode out. No time to lose.

"Mrs Frobisher—Diane—I'm so sorry for your loss. First your husband, and now your daughter. I can't imagine how you must be feeling, but unfortunately I do have to ask you some questions, and every second counts. Is that all right?"

She nodded, but she was still in shock and I had the feeling she had no real idea what was happening. The Reverend Enoch Williams slid a protective arm around Diane's shoulders and clutched her hand more tightly. She didn't seem to notice, perched in brittle stillness on the edge of the brown leather sofa.

I lowered my voice. "Diane, can you think of anyone who would want to harm Chelsea? Did she have any enemies? Former boyfriends, anyone who was jealous of her position at the hospital? She was awfully young to be a consultant, wasn't she?"

Diane shrugged. Her faded blue eyes were distant and she seemed to be having difficulty focusing.

Reverend Williams said, "Can't these questions wait? I knew Chelsea as well as anybody—she was my churchwarden after all—and I can assure you she was universally loved. She was a good Christian girl. It must have been a random attack—someone off the street who happened to wander into church at the wrong moment."

Girl? She was at least thirty-two. Random attack? I stifled the urge to laugh at his naivety. "Why would a stranger choose to harm her, Reverend?"

His smile froze as his complexion turned a deeper shade of puce. He retreated into bluster. "The safe is in the vestry. Perhaps he thought he could get at money, perhaps she caught him breaking in and stopped him. Perhaps he didn't like the look of her. Perhaps he was a pervert—I don't know! You're the detective, you work it out."

He glanced at Diane, but she failed to respond other than to push back behind her ear a strand of straying grey hair, with a sudden, impatient gesture.

I moistened my lips and deliberately addressed myself to her. "You see, Diane, in my line of work we're always suspicious of coincidences, and it is a huge coincidence that your husband and your daughter died in the same week."

It was harsh, but it brought a puzzled frown to her brow. "Chelsea was hit on the head. Robert died from a heart attack. How can they possibly be connected—other than the family connection, of course?"

"Chelsea was Robert's step-daughter, I believe? Did they get on? Any problems between them?"

A small shudder ran through her slender frame and her voice was bitter. "As you well know, Chelsea inherited from Robert. He left me the house for my lifetime and a small allowance, but the bulk went to Chelsea, plus this house when I go. Does that answer your question?"

I raised my eyebrows but forbore to comment. It sounded like an odd arrangement, but now was not the time to probe. All the same, I wondered whether the only relationship between Chelsea and Robert was step-daughter and step-father, given that Robert was ten years younger than his wife. And who inherited now that Chelsea was dead?

I turned to the rector. "Reverend Williams, I know you've already answered questions about Robert Frobisher's death, but indulge me." I added a winning smile but the rector was unmoved, so I ploughed on. "Did you see him collapse? Did anyone else touch the organ console? Did you

POISONED BY YEW AND OTHER STORIES

notice anyone dusting the keys afterwards?"

"Dusting the keys?" He stared at me as though I was mad. "When our organist had just dropped dead? We were all far too busy calling the ambulance and praying for poor Robert, to be concerned with cleaning. And yes, as a matter of fact I observed it all. Robert had just sat down at the console, changed his shoes—he wears special shoes with thin soles so that he can feel the pedals—and unlocked the lid. He placed his hands on the keys to start playing and that was it. A mighty crash as his head hit the keyboards, and he was gone. We dragged him off the stool and laid him on the floor in order to begin resuscitation, but it was no good. The paramedics were there within ten minutes with their electrical apparatus, but to no avail. It was shocking."

My lips quirked at the unintentional pun, but I kept my expression suitably sombre. "Who helped to lift him from the organ stool?"

He began to count off on pudgy fingers. "Well, let's see. There was Andy Grossman—he's my other churchwarden, Chelsea's counterpart— Jane Hillier, my curate, Bob Hunter, the verger—he has arms like an ox, he's a gardener—and Tony Lessing, the treasurer. Oh, and poor Chelsea herself. Naturally, she was very upset. Fortunately not many of the congregation had arrived. Robert always starts to play—used to start to play—fifteen minutes before the service begins, but most of the congregation arrive within the last few minutes." He added this with a sort of sniff, making clear his opinion of those who arrived at the final moment.

"I shall need a list of all their names and addresses. Who closed the organ?"

"What?" He looked confused. "I've no idea. Why? Is it important?"

"I'm afraid it is." I looked at Diane. "Your husband didn't die from natural causes, Diane. We have evidence to suggest he was murdered."

"Murdered?" All colour left her face and her mouth opened wide.

I thought she was going to faint, so I kept talking in a low, even voice. "We have evidence to show that your husband died from acute mercury poisoning. We believe dimethyl mercury—it's a colourless liquid, so undetectable apart from a very slight sweet smell—was painted on the organ keys. It's highly toxic and absorbed through the skin. Did either of you notice anyone wearing thick gardening gloves immediately prior to the service?"

They looked at each other and shook their heads. The rector said, "You could ask Bob. He'd notice anything like that, being a gardener himself. Anyway, I don't see what any of this has to do with poor Chelsea being hit on the head."

I stood up. "We're working on that. Thank you both for your time. I'll see myself out."

The interview hadn't got me much further, and to make matters worse, the next time I saw Jack he held up a pair of frilly black knickers, about the size to fit a flea.

"I'm nearly there," he taunted, "so I thought I might as well start on the shopping."

I glared at him. "If you think I'm wearing those, you've another think coming. As I've told you before, Dr. Death, you stick to your forensics and let the detectives detect, if you don't mind."

He chortled at that, but apart from telling me there were no unexpected fingerprints at the scene of either crime, refused to share any further information with me.

My team worked hard over the next few days, questioning all those who were present at Robert's death, and any who had access to the vestry, where Chelsea had been killed by a blow to the back of the head with—yes, you've guessed—a heavy brass candlestick.

We unearthed some interesting facts. Bob Hunter, the gardening verger, had several pairs of thick gardening gloves and some face masks, as well as mercury compounds used in fertiliser, stashed away in his shed. He claimed to have forgotten about the fertiliser, which he last used about forty years ago, but since the shed was neater than my kitchen (okay, that's not saying much) I hesitated to believe him. We took the lot away for Jack to analyse.

The curate, Jane Hillier, soon became what we call in the trade a person of interest. Around forty-five years old, tall, strong, and somewhat austere in manner, she had changed careers after experiencing some kind of religious conversion. Prior to her training at theological college and her first post here as curate, she had been a chemistry teacher in a girls' high school. She was terrifyingly religious—not too surprising, I suppose, given her calling—but that kind of fanaticism worries me. She told me a shade too quickly that she never liked Robert Frobisher.

"He was a control freak," she snapped. "Practically ran the church. Everyone walked on eggshells around him. Pandered to his every whim."

"And?"

"And he refused point blank to play anything modern. I ask you! How can you expect to get new people into church if all the hymns are pre-1930? I'm sorry he's gone and all that, and I'm holding his widow very much in my prayers, but to be honest with you, Detective Chief Inspector, we're going to be a whole lot better off without him. He was a very unpleasant man. Not a proper Christian."

I blinked. "I see. Does Reverend Williams share your views?"

She snorted, reminding me for a moment of the chestnut filly in the field next to our home. "He'd never admit to it. Claims to like all that old stuff, but the church is half empty. How he gets on in his chaplaincy at the university, I'll never know! He'll soon change his tune though, when the church starts filling up with new families learning to love the Lord Jesus Christ as their Saviour."

Her auburn eyes glittered fervently and I took a step back. "You taught chemistry to 'A' level prior to your vocation to the priesthood? What do you know about dimethyl mercury?"

"Highly toxic. There was a famous case of a research chemist in 1997, Karen Wetterhahn. She took all the proper precautions, but a few drops of the stuff dripped onto her latex glove. She was dead within six months."

"The effects are not immediate, then?"

"Can be. Depends how much is absorbed. One spray would be sufficient for instantaneous death. Why are you asking me all this?"

When I told her, she folded her hands, lifted her eyes to heaven and started to pray. I beat a hasty retreat.

Andy Grossman, the other churchwarden, had the usual cautious air of any successful solicitor, but he answered my questions willingly enough. "I was at the other end of the church preparing to hand out hymn books when I heard the crash. I and Tony—that's Tony Lessing, our treasurer, he's a farmer—helped to lift poor Robert from the stool and lay him on the ground. Then we did mouth-to-mouth and heart massage. We didn't let up until the ambulance arrived. It was too late, though. He'd already passed on to his heavenly home."

I resisted the urge to roll my eyes. "Did you notice who closed the organ?"

"Well it might have been—no, he was over the other side—perhaps it was—but it can't have been, can it? I'm sure Chelsea would have remembered. Such a terrible thing. She was so clever, you know. Very observant. Chelsea would have noticed, but I'm sorry. I'm afraid I didn't, I was too busy. She did look kind of quizzical, though, I do remember that. Chelsea, that is."

He smiled, so I smiled back. "That's all right. Tell me, is Tony Lessing still farming?"

"Oh yes. He has that big grain farm to the east of the village. They export everywhere. He's very successful, but I'm afraid he didn't much care for Robert. None of us did; he was a difficult man. He and Tony had a big argument, everyone heard it. Robert accused him of price fixing and not unnaturally Tony became very upset. It was becoming so ugly I was forced to intervene and warn Robert of the slander laws. It was only a week before Robert died, so I expect Tony feels bad now."

Especially if he murdered him. "Thank you, Andy. You've been most helpful."

Back at the station I did my best to avoid Jack the pathologist—he was the last person I wished to see—but inevitably he tracked me down, this time waving in my face a frothy black bra which would barely hold a couple of walnuts. His eyes were gleaming.

"Don't get your hopes up," I told him. "It's not over yet. I'm on the point of obtaining a confession."

"And just how, sweetie pie, are you planning to do that?"

Corny, I know, but I tapped the side of my nose. "You don't deserve it, but because I'm a truly lovely person, I'll tell you anyway. I'm having an Aggie Christie showdown at six o'clock tonight."

He roared with laughter. Wiping the tears from his eyes he spluttered, "No, come on, Miss Marple. Tell me what you're really doing. You haven't any idea who did it, have you?"

I smiled. "The murderer will be in custody by—" I glanced at my watch, "—six-thirty tonight. And then, my dear Dr. Death, you will definitely need to watch your back."

They were all gathered in the vestry when I arrived at six, Diane Frobisher, still pallid but a little more in control of herself, Jane Hillier and Enoch Williams, Tony Lessing, Andy Grossman, and Bob Hunter. They were nervous and wide-eyed, which was to my advantage. It was a gamble, but I reckoned any churchgoer with two murders on his or her conscience would be only too ready to spill the beans and cleanse the soul, given enough pressure. Choosing the venue of the vestry, where the second murder took place, and within sight of the organ console was, though I say it myself, an act of genius guaranteed to unsettle. The atmosphere was charged.

I began without preamble. "You all know why you're here; because every one of you is a suspect in the murders of Robert Frobisher and his step-daughter. Do any of you wish to tell me anything?" I stared at each of them in turn, but they all dropped their eyes.

I let the silence linger until they were clearly uncomfortable, then I said, "Very few murders are committed without cause, so our primary focus has been to look for motive. All of you here had some sort of motive to murder Robert Frobisher, and since the poison was applied to the organ keys well before the start of the Sunday service, you all had opportunity."

They all looked resentful at this unwarranted impeachment of their Christian characters. Some of them gasped. Andy Grossman showed a fighting spark. "I don't think I had a motive, and anyway, what about Chelsea? Presumably the same person committed both murders, so what would be the motive to murder her?"

I extinguished the spark. "Chelsea was killed because she saw something incriminating. As a doctor she was trained to be observant—you told me so yourself—and she saw something which puzzled her. She spotted one of you closing the organ lid while everyone else was attending to Robert. With a poison so toxic, it was essential that the organ lid be closed before anyone else touched the keys. Since Robert was assumed to have died from natural causes, there was plenty of time to come back later and clean the keys properly. I think Chelsea confronted the murderer here in the vestry, and was killed to prevent her talking."

Jane Hillier was still glaring daggers, and even Enoch Williams looked hostile.

I pressed my advantage. "I understand you're married to a pharmacist, Mr. Grossman, so you'd know all about poisons and their effects. That puts you in the centre of the frame. As for you two," I turned my attention to Tony Lessing and Bob Hunter, "you both deal with fungicides. You, Tony, had a row with Robert shortly before his death, and you, Bob, had all the equipment necessary for Robert's murder. Mind you," I swept the rest of them with a stern gaze, "any one of you could have rifled Bob's shed and used his stuff."

"What about me? I presume I'm some sort of suspect too?"

"You certainly are, Reverend Hillier. You made no secret of your dislike of Robert Frobisher, and until recently you taught chemistry. Oh yes. You're definitely there. And you too, Reverend Williams, with your background as chaplain to the university. It wouldn't have required too much ingenuity to snaffle a sample of dimethyl mercury from the labs. And from all accounts, Robert Frobisher held some sort of power over you."

The rector said, "You surely can't suspect Diane of killing her own daughter?"

I thought carefully before I answered. "I'm afraid Diane had the best motive of all—money—that, coupled with a growing hatred of her husband and resentment of her daughter's relationship with him, puts her high on the list."

By the hostile glances and the jutting lips, I could sense they were at the point of exploding with righteous indignation, so I played the joker. I swung round to face the grieving widow and mother.

"Diane Frobisher, I am arresting you on the charge of murder. You have the right to remain—"

"Stop it at once! Stop this farce. Diane is completely innocent. I killed Robert Frobisher, and his step-daughter." The Reverend Enoch Williams stepped forward, his face pale but determined. He turned to Diane with a look of anguish. "Don't you see, my darling, I had to do it. That hateful man—I couldn't watch you suffering any longer. And knowing that your own daughter was colluding with him—it was too much. I've loved you for so long, Diane. I did it for us. I'm sorry about Chelsea—she was a good churchwarden and a good doctor—but she knew too much and she was cheating on you with your own husband. That sort of evil has to be stamped out. You do see that, don't you?"

By the look of horror on Diane Frobisher's face, I doubt she saw anything. And I doubt his feelings had ever been reciprocated. The others were all regarding him askance, with similar expressions of incredulity and disgust. I arrested the Reverend Enoch Williams and took him away without any sign of a struggle.

Later that evening after supper I found myself clad only in a pair of very brief, black lacy panties and a minuscule black bra. But I got my own back, for my husband was stripped down to nothing but a union jack thong. They say husband and wife teams shouldn't work together, but I don't know. I think there's something to be said for it after all. Especially when you're married to the best pathologist in the business.

7 BATS IN THE BELFRY

For once I was there first, but I quickly turned away from the gruesome sight. Unlike Jack, the doctor of death, I've never appreciated the attraction of dead bodies. This one, with the thick rope still twisted around his neck, had a bloated, crimson face with a swollen tongue protruding from his bloodless lips, and staring, sightless eyes practically popping out of his head. The wisps of thinning grey hair carefully combed across the top of his skull were so incongruous that I nearly laughed out loud, but one look at the chalk-white visage of the young constable—surely no more than twenty years old—who had called it in and was standing by my side, restrained me. I glared at him instead.

"Where is that darned pathologist?" I barked. "Never here when you need him. Ring him again, Constable."

"Er, ma'am, I only rang him five minutes ago. He said he'd be half an hour. Should I—oh, yes, ma'am. Right away."

"And stay downstairs in the church," I yelled at his rapidly retreating back. "Nobody is to come up here other than the scene of crime guys. Do you understand? Nobody."

After a cursory glance around the belfry I averted my eyes. Nothing much to see, apart from the deceased, and I'd already seen quite enough of him, thank you.

I was still standing there thinking, when a bright voice greeted me. "Detective Chief Inspector, as I live and die! Fancy meeting you here. What delights are you offering me today?"

I hid my relief. No point in increasing his sense of superiority. "About time too! What kept you?"

"Well now," he began to count off on his fingers. "There was the liver from number two—cirrhosis, I regret to say, so enlarged and yellow with plenty of necrotic nodules—then there were the breasts from that young teenager with the overdose. They were—"

"—yes, thank you, Doctor. That's more than sufficient detail. Just get on with the task in hand. When did this man die? Suicide or murder?"

Jack's face assumed that pseudo-serious expression I know so well. He only does it to annoy me. "Detective Chief Inspector! I couldn't possibly comment on whether or not it was murder. That's your field, not mine. Mere mortals like me simply report the facts."

I ground my teeth. "And the facts in this case are?"

"I'm coming to that. No need to poop your panties, darling. Give me a chance. Let me see. He's been dead around four hours. At first sight I'd say he died of strangulation by bell rope, but look. Come here. See these bruises here on his upper arms? Almost certainly caused by someone gripping him—perhaps to heft him up into this crude noose? Oh! Look at this!" He pronounced with an air of delighted glee. "At the back of his head here, see? He's had a glancing blow. Probably not enough to kill him since it hasn't bled much, but more than likely it would have stunned him. You're the detective. You decide. In view of the bruises and the blow on the head, was it suicide or murder, sweetheart?"

"All right, no need for your juvenile jokes, Dr Death. Surely even you know that sarcasm is the lowest form of wit?"

"And the highest form of humour," he rejoined. "Anyway, that's about it for now. As far as I'm concerned, you can cut him down and send him back to my lab any time you want. And I'll see you later, DCI, just in case there's anything else you want."

"I shouldn't set your hopes too high on that score," I growled, as he made his way back down the winding stone steps. I do like to get in the last word now and again.

The Reverend Montague Brighton, vicar of the parish, identified the deceased as the tower captain, the guy responsible for organising the bell ringers and the campanology.

"As far as you know, did Mr Benson have any enemies?"

The Reverend Montague hesitated for a little too long. "No—o, not really. No, of course not."

"But?"

"You must understand, Aidan Benson wasn't a church attender. Ringing was his passion, not God. So I didn't know him all that well."

"But?"

His shoulders slumped. "I hate to speak ill of the dead, but I have to say he wasn't entirely popular. Didn't encourage the youngsters, and was quite irascible at times. He was a perfectionist, so he used to get rather angry when the ringers failed to produce perfection which, if I'm honest, was most of the time."

"You discovered the body, I understand?"

"That's right. The ringers either go home or across to another tower, at the start of the morning service. Aidan is always the last to leave, since he's responsible for the state of the belfry. He's very conscientious. Everything has to be exactly so before he leaves."

"Who would have seen him leave?"

The vicar shrugged. "Probably no one. I see some of the ringers leave as I wait at the west end to begin the walk up the aisle at the start of the service, but I don't notice exactly who leaves or when. I don't even know who is here to ring. There are around a dozen in the team but only six bells, so you never know who is going to ring on any particular day. I expect Aidan kept a rota or something, but that was his territory. Nothing to do with me. And I'm the last person to walk up the aisle. The congregation is all seated before I begin my perambulation, so I doubt anyone even thought about the ringers."

"Do you know of anyone who disliked Aidan Benson enough to murder him?"

I asked it brutally, and the vicar flinched. He replied with a touch of acerbity. "No I don't. I've told you all I know, so if you don't mind... It's been a long day."

"Of course, Vicar. Thank you for your help. I'll call on Mrs Benson next. She may be able to furnish me with a list of ringers."

I thought he stiffened slightly, but it may have been my imagination.

Amalie Benson was a revelation. I guess I'd been expecting a match to her ageing, discontented, recently deceased husband. Not a bit of it. Amalie Benson was tall, willowy, and very elegant. With long, slender legs which tapered into the neatest ankles I've ever seen, shown off to great advantage by red stilettos, she exuded quality. I put her age somewhere in the early forties, although Botox may have borne some responsibility for that. Goodness knows what had induced her to marry Aidan. I can't imagine he was ever particularly dashing.

She was perfectly poised and in full control of her emotions. Indeed, she made no attempt at pretence, and I admired her for her honesty.

"His manner of death is a terrible shock, of course it is," she said quietly, "but we'd led separate lives for years. He's wedded to bell ringing, not to me."

I must have raised my eyebrows, for she continued, "No need to look like that, Chief Inspector. I discovered soon after our marriage that Aidan's—er—interests lay in a different direction, and not only in ringing bells, if you get my meaning."

"You mean he was gay?"

"I'm afraid so, although that word is something of a misnomer in Aidan's case. Gay he never was. Miserable, moody and morose, yes. Gay, no."

"So did you—um—cast your eyes elsewhere?"

An ironic gleam crept into her sultry eyes. "Delicately put, Chief Inspector. I didn't remain a virgin for the whole of my married life, if that's what you mean."

"Why not get divorced?"

She shrugged and spread her hands. "For what? I have a comfortable home here, and Aidan and I rubbed along together pretty well, as long as we kept out of each other's way. The arrangement suited both of us. Neither of us asked too many questions."

"I'm afraid I must ask questions, though, since this is a murder enquiry. I need the names of all your lovers for, let's say, the last five years. And I need to know your own movements this morning."

She smiled outright at that, but it was a mocking smile. "I've been here all day, with no witnesses. As for a list of my lovers, I don't think you can compel me to do that. No, Chief Inspector. You must find that out for yourself."

She might have left me struggling, had not the telephone rung at that very moment. She turned her back on me to answer it, but not before I spotted her face light up.

When she came off the phone she said, "That was the vicar, in case you're wondering. Dear Monty. He's been such a support. He's coming round. Such a comfort."

"I'll take my leave, then. Thank you for your help, Mrs Benson."

She said, "I don't know that I've been much help to you."

Now it was my turn to smile enigmatically.

When I reached home the best pathologist in the business was cooking liver and onions. I tried not to remember what he had told me earlier on about liver. Of course, he does it deliberately just to see my reaction. I try not to show it.

"How's the case coming along, my sweet?" he asked, in the sort of tone which suggested he expected me to have no idea whatsoever.

"Oh," I said airily, "I shall be making two arrests first thing tomorrow. Case solved."

Jack's eyes widened. "What? You can't!"

"Excuse me, but I think I can! It was the vicar and Amalie Benson. They've been having an affair for years, I'm sure of it. Amalie couldn't divorce Aidan because the scandal would finish Monty Brighton's career, so Monty slipped up to the belfry when all the ringers had gone, bashed Aidan on the head, dragged him over to the rope and hanged him. Simple, my dear Watson."

Jack seemed duly impressed. "Are you absolutely certain, Sherlock?"

I nodded, trying hard not to smirk. "I am, Doctor."

He grinned, a grin which spread right across his face. He took me in his arms and hugged me. Then he murmured against my hair, "I'm sorry to disappoint you, sweetie, but it was an accident, and I can prove it. There was no murder. Bats roost in that belfry. Bat droppings on Aidan's clothing show that they became active while he was there, and this can only have been after the bells had finished. I think a bat swooped, and startled Aidan. He slipped, hit his head on the wall, and caught his foot in the end of the rope which somehow got tangled round his neck. Remember, he was stunned at the time. In fighting to free himself, he simply managed to pull the rope tighter. I'm afraid it was nothing but a terrible accident, DCI."

"Ha!" I said, twisting out of his arms. "Haven't you forgotten the bruises on Aidan's upper arms? You said they were the result of someone holding him."

"Like this?" He grabbed me by the arms, and I found myself melting towards him. "Caused during love making, my sweet, but with no criminal intent."

Then he licked his finger and drew a large one in the air. "I think that's one up to me, don't you, DCI?"

Somehow I didn't mind too much. I liked Amalie Benson and that old rogue, the Reverend Montague Brighton, and I wished them well. Besides, I had an idea my forfeit might perhaps be quite good fun.

8 GREEN MURDER

"A green murder, this one!"

There are times when Jack drives me demented. He may be the best pathologist in the business, but he's emotionally challenged, his development having arrested at puberty. He takes great pride in wearing one of those awful 'NFN' tee shirts under his greens—Normal For Norfolk—probably because he knows how much it irritates me, a Norfolk daughter.

I purse my lips, but I'm forced to play his silly game. "Green?"

"Just one blow to the head with the proverbial blunt instrument, then shoved under the compost heap and left to rot. From dust you came and to dust you shall return. No serial killer, this. IMHO, an impulse murder by someone who panicked, but who disposed of the body in an environmentally friendly manner."

"Spare me the conjecture and the quotes! Anything else? Anything I can actually use? Material, shape of blunt instrument?"

"Ouch! Tetchy! No need to get your knickers in a twist over this one, Detective Chief Inspector. Should be simple enough to solve, even for you. There's an indentation on the left temple which I'm not yet able to classify, but before you ask, I'm working on it. Let you know, sweetheart, as soon as I do.

"Bearing in mind the heat from the compost and the growth of weeds under the decomposed remains, I estimate he was killed around three months ago. Can't be any more accurate than that. Thirty-four year old male, poor dental care but he had seen a dentist at least once in his life, so should be easy to identify. Plenty of DNA, so no problem for a woman of your calibre."

I narrowed my eyes at him. "Any DNA from the perp?"

"'Fraid not, DCI Brooks. No helpful clues from the murderer. Something interesting, though." His eyes gleamed expectantly.

"It's not a TV game show, Jack. Just tell me."

He sighed, exaggeratedly. "You're no fun any more. Look." He held a tiny gem in the palm of his hand. "It's a diamond. Good one, too. I reckon this guy was part of a diamond heist and—"

"—thank you, Jack. Just concentrate on the forensics and leave the detecting to the detectives, will you?"

There are times when it's good to be a detective in Norfolk. Mostly our work is in Norwich or Yarmouth or Thetford, so taking a leisurely drive to a tiny country church out in the fields is like a day off, especially in early summer when that wide, Norfolk sky is azure blue and the air is sweet and fresh.

The rector and his tiny band of church devotees were waiting for me, as arranged. All eight of them looked to be aged about a hundred, what with their walking sticks and grey heads and rheumatic joints, but I noticed a few pairs of ancient male eyes intent upon my legs as I changed from my high heels to a pair of wellies. Not quite dead yet, then.

"Don't get up," I said to the three adorning the bench against the south wall of the flint-knapped church. "Lovely day, isn't it?"

The stout old bat dressed in a tweed suit despite the sunshine, looked down her nose. "I hardly think a violent death can be described as 'lovely'," she huffed. "It was my Rusty who first alerted us. Naturally I had to take the bone away from him, and I don't think he's quite forgiven me."

I glanced at the mournful spaniel lying at her feet. It was so fat it could hardly bring itself to raise its head, let alone wag its tail. I bent down to pet it.

"Be careful," warned the old bat. "He doesn't like strangers."

I had a feeling it wasn't only the dog who didn't like strangers. Eight pairs of rheumy eyes were regarding me balefully.

Clearly the friendly approach was failing. I adopted what that darned pathologist calls my 'officious voice'. "Rector, can you take me through the events of Thursday?"

He glanced nervously at the old bat, then his eyes switched to his churchwarden, who gave an infinitesimal nod of encouragement. "I—er—Mrs. Trumble here brought it to my attention. She used to be matron of the cottage hospital years ago, so she knows about bones. She recognised it immediately as being human, didn't you, Mabel?"

The old bat graciously inclined her head.

"That's it, really. Horace here—that's Major Wilkins, he's our churchwarden—he said we must call the police, so we did."

"We didn't touch nuffin'."

I turned to the new speaker. "And you are?"

27

"Oh, I'm sorry," said the rector. "Let me introduce us. I've already mentioned Mrs Trumble and Major Wilkins." He moved round the group from left to right, starting with the recent speaker. "This is George Adams—he was our butcher when we had a butcher's shop in the village. Sadly, it's long gone now. Adrian Harkness, retired schoolmaster. Olivia and Eric Bunn—the Bunns have farmed here for generations. Maurice Catchpole—he was the bank manager until the local branch closed. That was in 1982. And I'm the Reverend Clark Gable. I've been here forty years."

With a supreme effort, I kept my face straight. "Did any of you know the victim?"

There was a pause, and again that fleeting glance between them. Adrian Harkness, the schoolmaster, spoke up. "Oh yes, we all knew Vincent. One of my pupils, and a very troubled soul, I'm sorry to say."

I raised my eyebrows.

He continued, "He came to church regularly, with his grandmother. He was in the choir, when we had a choir. That was when there were rather more people in church than there are today. Vincent lived with his grandmother after his parents were killed in a car crash when he was eight. Terrible tragedy." He shook his head dolefully, and the others adopted similar expressions of sorrow. "I'm afraid young Vincent got into trouble with you police. Nothing serious, just a bit of shoplifting and joyriding, but it finished his grandma. She died soon after, and that was the last we saw of Vincent. He was taken into care, and none of us have seen him from that day to this."

"You didn't follow him up, keep in touch?" I addressed the rector.

An expression of guilt flitted across his face. He gazed at the ground.

Mrs Trumble rode to his rescue. "The rector can't be expected to follow up every child that moves away. He's kept very busy looking after his flock."

All eight nodded solemnly, like one of those Chinese dolls.

"How big is your flock, Father?"

This time it was Eric Bunn who rushed to his aid. "It's not so big now, of course. This is an estate church, built in the fifteenth century for the farm workers. That's why it's in a field, a mile and a half outside the village. Nowadays, the estate is managed by the farmer—that's our son, James— and one other man. Times have changed. So now there's just the eight of us in Clark's 'flock', as you put it."

"It's very peaceful," I remarked, listening to the bird song and the lowing of the cattle in the next field. "Can any of you think of a reason why Vincent might have come back here?"

Again, that surreptitious glance. Major Wilkins spoke up. "We have no idea."

"It would be feasible to imagine that he came to meet somebody. Why else would he show up in a remote place like this?"

George Adams growled, "He were a bad lot, that lad. 'Spect he came to meet a drug dealer or suffin'."

"A drug dealer? Here?" I endeavoured to keep the incredulity from my voice. "Sounds like you had experience of young Vincent?"

His already florid complexion turned a darker shade of puce. "Stole from me, he did. Used him as a butcher's boy, to deliver meat an' that, but the bugger pocketed the cash. I ain't got no time for the likes of him."

Little Mrs Bunn, one of those elderly beige types who generally blend in with the background, nodded a little too fervently. "Vincent wasn't very nice. He bullied poor James at school, didn't he, Adrian?"

"I had to keep the boy under control," the schoolmaster admitted. "Very disruptive element in class. To be honest, I was glad when he left. Not that I didn't feel sorry for him," he hastened to add, "coping with all those deaths, but I had the other children to consider. I had a duty to them."

I was about to enquire whether Mrs Trumble had known the victim, when she volunteered with another look down that long nose, "Dreadful boy. Vicious streak in him. Unkind to animals. Do you know, I once caught him throwing stones at a cat. I'm not ashamed to say I think he deserved all he got."

She glared at me with an expression of such defiance that I backed off, turning instead to the final member of the group, former bank manager Maurice Catchpole. "And you, Mr Catchpole? Did you know Vincent?"

There was just a hint of hesitation before he replied, "Only slightly, I'm afraid. Boys like that don't use banks!" He laughed, nervously. "I met him that time when he vandalised the church, but that's all."

"Vandalised the church?"

"It wasn't much," the rector said. "Damaged a few hymn books and left empty crisp packets and cigarette ash on the high altar. That's all."

I'd never seen a heaving bosom until then. Mabel Trumble was a picture of righteous indignation. "Nearly set the church on fire with his smoking. You're much too forgiving, Clark."

"Seventy times seven, Mabel. Let us not forget our Lord's wonderful words."

"Clark," she gushed, "you're a model for us all. We're so fortunate to have you as our rector and friend, guiding us in the way we should go."

They nodded in unison. What a nauseating bunch of geriatric hypocrites! I was beginning to feel the need to throw up. Instead, I asked casually, "Where would I find the nearest jeweller?"

They looked confused by the abrupt change of topic, but were suddenly anxious to please.

"There's one in Norwich—"

"Try Castle Mall."

"The antiques man in the market—"

"Maurice makes it. He's a brilliant jeweller, aren't you, Maurice?"

"Only a hobby," Maurice Catchpole demurred. "I'm not a professional."

"But he does lovely work." Olivia Bunn struggled to unfasten the crucifix around her neck.

I examined it with interest. "That's beautiful. I love that single diamond in the centre."

"Maurice's trademark," Olivia told me, as proud as if she fashioned the jewellery herself. "We all have some little piece with a diamond."

Indeed? I rummaged in my briefcase and withdrew the diamond found at the scene of the crime. I showed it to Maurice Catchpole. "Is this one of yours?"

His eyes widened in alarm. "Where did you find that?"

"Underneath the body. I think what happened was this." All eyes were upon me. "Vincent arranged to meet someone he knew from the past, perhaps one of you. There was an argument which threatened to develop into a fight. Whoever met with Vincent swung at him with whatever came to hand, happened to catch him on the temple and killed him—a lucky blow. The perpetrator panicked and hid the body in the nearest spot, the compost heap, but in so doing, lost a diamond. Now, are you going to tell me who killed Vincent, or am I going to have to take you all into custody and charge you as accessories?"

There was a collective gasp. The tired faces seemed to crumple, but stalwart Mabel Trumble spoke out. "You're very clever, Detective Chief Inspector. We didn't expect you to work it out so quickly. The truth is, we're all in it together and none of us will tell you who struck the fatal blow. You see, that young man terrorised this area for years. He made all our lives a misery. We tried to help him, but he was non-responsive. We thanked God when Vincent was taken into care. We were all here clearing the churchyard when he suddenly reappeared. He started again, threatening and abusing us. I'm afraid it dragged up all those painful memories, and we couldn't face it, not at our time of life. One of us lashed out, and unfortunately he died."

"Why didn't you call the police, if it was an accident?"

The rector said apologetically, "We panicked. We thought if no one knew he was here, no one would come looking for him, so we buried him under the compost. We held a little service over him and I said a prayer. Then, when nothing happened, it was if it had all gone away—until Rusty found the bone. Then we knew we must tell the authorities."

"Don't leave home," I warned, as I climbed back into my car. "I haven't decided yet how to charge you, but I'll be back."

"Easy-peasy," I boasted, as I sailed into the home I share with my husband. I gave him a triumphant peck on the cheek. "Solved it in an hour, but I don't think there'll be a case to answer. Self-defence."

I didn't notice the sombre look on his face. He held me tight. "Sweetheart, there may be a problem."

"What?"

"While you were enjoying a jolly in the country, a guy called James Bunn came into the station. He's a local farmer. He told us about a village paedophile ring; church, primary school, butcher's shop, bank. Guess where it is?"

"No!" I whispered. "Not those harmless old fools? Please tell me it's not them?"

Jack nodded. "Afraid so. And apparently one of the most hapless victims was a very good looking young boy by the name of Vincent, who came back to confront them..."

I shuddered. "I'll have them all, even though the schoolmaster actually murdered him."

"How do you know that?"

"He had a white band on his ring finger where he'd removed his ring. And he uses a walking stick with a brass top in the shape of a dog's head."

My husband, the best pathologist in the business, nodded slowly. "That fits. Go get 'em, cowgirl."

So I did.

9 POISONED BY YEW

"Definitely one for you, darling. Come closer, my sweet."

I hovered by the door, stifling the urge to gag at the stench as Jack, that miserable excuse for a human being, deliberately emptied the stomach contents into a stainless steel bowl. He may be the best pathologist in the business, but on occasions he goes too far. This was one of them.

I pulled a tissue from my pocket and held it over my nose. "Just tell me how she died, Jack. I'm not in the mood for your childish attempt at humour."

He wasn't in the least abashed. "Knickers in a twist again, Detective Chief Inspector?" He held the bowl to his nose and sniffed loudly. "Hm. Spag bol followed by strawberry ice cream, unless I'm much mistaken."

Feeling myself turning green and in danger of losing my breakfast, I leaned against the door jamb for support. "Jack!"

"Oh, all right. Have it your way. You're no fun any more, DCI. I need to do some more tests, but by the distension of her stomach and the inflammation of the mucosae, I'd say she was poisoned."

I averted my eyes. "How and when?"

"Death within an hour of ingesting yew."

"Yew? How on earth would a human being ingest yew?"

A broad, self-satisfied grin spread across his face until I yearned to slap him. "Looks like an infusion. My guess is that someone gave her a cup of yew tea, but as you're so fond of telling me, Detective Chief Inspector, you're the cop. I'm merely the pathologist."

"Well—don't forget it, then!" was the best I could manage as I made a hasty exit.

When I looked up yew poisoning on the internet, I discovered that a few leaves could kill a cow in less than eight hours. Since our victim was not much more than five foot three and weighed a mere six stone, I imagine a nice mug of herbal tea proffered by a friendly peasant would offer her little chance of longevity. The poor kid probably lived just long enough to stagger into the churchyard, which I guess is a sensible enough place to end your days.

But who would want to murder young Cherry Pye, and why?

I started with her last foster home, where loud, thumping music could be heard from upstairs. Mabel Poynter was a pillar of the local church. As well as fostering three teenagers, she was what's known these days as a 'worship leader', which means she led what passes as church services in trendy places, accompanied by drums and guitars and God knows what else.

A middle-aged woman of generous proportions, Mabel's eyes welled up when I broke the sad news. "Not our Cherry! Please, this is a joke, right? Please tell me it's not true."

"I'm sorry, Mrs Poynter. Can you tell me why you failed to report her missing?"

Her shoulders heaved. "I blame myself. If only I'd rung you people right at the outset, but I didn't want to get her into any more trouble. The courts threatened her with detention if she violated her probation again, and I just wanted to give her another chance. She—um—she had found her way onto the streets, I'm afraid. She made good money out of prostitution and didn't like giving it up when the courts found out she was under age. She resented being sent into foster care, even though we did our best for her. She was a lovely girl, underneath that hard exterior."

I pictured that frail, vulnerable body on Jack's slab. "Had she gone missing before?"

"She—er—wasn't much of a home bird, to be honest. We did our best, Gavin and me, but it can be difficult when you don't get them until they're teenagers. We really tried. Gave her a lot of love and took her to church with us, just like a proper happy family. She seemed to enjoy the services. They're lovely services, bright and exciting. Just right for teenagers."

I began to feel even more sorry for little Cherry Pye. "Where is Gavin now?"

"Oh!" A hand flew to her mouth. "He's out looking for Cherry. I'd better ring him."

"No, don't do that, Mrs Poynter. We'll contact him. I need to speak with your other foster children."

She started to argue, but a look at my face convinced her otherwise. She heaved herself off the sofa and yelled up the stairs. When that produced no observable result, she plodded up the stairs to reappear a few moments later with two skinny, spotty teenagers in tow.

"This is Mandy—Mandy Sheppard—and this is Jimmy Baxter. Say hello to the Detective Chief Inspector, you two."

They muttered something indiscernible and sat huddled together on the sofa, staring at the floor.

"Good morning, Mandy, Jimmy. I'm sorry about your friend. Cherry was a friend, wasn't she? How well did you know her?"

They glanced at each and shrugged.

Mabel said, "Cat got your tongues? Answer the Chief Inspector."

I said, "Mabel, perhaps if we could have some coffee?" I nearly asked for tea, but just in case.

When she'd gone, I prepared for a cosy chat. "I need you to tell me anything you can about Cherry, so that we can catch her killer. Do you know when she left, or why?"

Again, that furtive glance. Then Mandy licked her lips. "She didn't like it here."

"Why not? Had she been here long?"

The boy snickered. "Too long. She hated it. All that church stuff they make us do, Cherry wouldn't stand for it. Said she had rights—although I dunno what rights you get in care. I never seen any."

"Anything else? Apart from the church stuff?"

"Yes. She—"

Just then the door opened and Mabel bustled in with the coffee. Mandy clamped her lips tight shut. We drank our coffee in silence, apart from Mabel's inconsequential chatter, but I pricked up my ears when she happened to mention that the churchwarden ran a health store in the church every Wednesday morning.

"So did—what did you say her name was? Ida Trumpington? Did Ida run her health store yesterday?"

Mabel nodded. "It's all Fair Trade goods. Coffee and tea and chocolate. Dried fruit, dates, all sorts of food that can be stored for a time."

"I see. Does she sell herbal teas?"

Mandy put in, "Yeah, all kinds. We're always getting them. Blackcurrant and raspberry and some horrible stuff—"

"That's enough, Mandy. If the Chief Inspector has finished with you two, why don't you run along?"

She looked inquiringly at me as she said it. I nodded. "I may have to talk to you again, but that's all for now, thank you."

They left without a word.

Ida Trumpington was a dear. I took to her immediately, although obviously I couldn't let that cloud my judgement. In my job, everyone's guilty until proven innocent. A little old lady with snowy white hair, she had eyes as sharp and bright as a sparrow, and clearly, she loved her church. I asked her about the Fair Trade store.

"It's more of a stall than a store, just a table where I sell Fair Trade goods. It makes a bit of money for the church and it puts cash into the pockets of the growers back in the developing world, rather than into the hands of the middle men. I don't make much, but I enjoy doing it. I meet so many different people, and they all have a story to tell."

I showed her a photo of Cherry. "Did this girl come to your stall?"

She fetched up a pair of reading glasses, hanging on a cord round her neck. "Let me see. That's the girl with the funny name, isn't it? She hated it. Told me I was the only person who hadn't laughed when she told them her name. Poor little Cherry Pye. She wasn't a happy girl."

"Do you know why?"

"She lost her mother at the age of twelve. She haunts the churchyard here, where her mother's buried. Why? She hasn't done anything stupid, has she?"

"Stupid?"

A look of concern filled her face. "I was always afraid—she didn't have the bounce for life that a girl of her age ought to have. It worried me."

"Ida, are you saying you think she was at risk of suicide?"

Ida hesitated. "Maybe. She hasn't, has she? Don't tell she's taken her own life?"

I patted her arm. "We don't know yet. I'm afraid we discovered her body late yesterday, but we don't know why she died."

Ida Trumpington's lined face sagged. Then something steely entered her eyes. "I'll help you all I can," she said. "Have you spoken to the rector? He should be your next port of call."

The Reverend Simon Shaw was riding round the rectory garden on a mower like a cowboy at a rodeo, a straw boater on his head. Sitting at a wrought iron table watching him, was a middle-aged man with very little hair and a large gut overflowing his belt. He didn't get up as I approached, but shaded his eyes with his hand.

"You must be the cop."

"I'm a detective chief inspector, yes. And you are?"

He held out a pudgy hand, damp with sweat. "Gavin Poynter, church treasurer and married to the delightful Mabel."

I suspected sarcasm, but it was difficult to tell. Simon Shaw completed his circuit of the lawn, climbed off the mower, shook my hand and introduced himself, before sinking into the chair next to Gavin. He poured a glass of lemonade from an old fashioned jug with a piece of muslin over the top to deter any marauding insects.

"How can I help you, Detective Chief Inspector?"

"Did you know Cherry Pye?"

He shook his head mournfully. "Terrible thing. Gavin was just telling me. A young girl that age. Terrible."

"I understand you were her foster father, Mr Poynter?"

"Call me Gavin. Yes, nice girl. Had her hard side, but underneath she was soft as putty. Like a kitten. Sometimes had her claws unsheathed, but didn't mean anything by it. Can't imagine why she did it. We did our best for her, me and Mabel, but sometimes you just can't help them."

He heaved an exaggerated sigh.

The rector was still looking sorrowful. "Of course, we'll bury her in consecrated ground. Poor Gavin here was worried about that, but the church changed its attitude long ago. We recognise now that suicide is a result of mental illness rather than wilful disobedience to God."

I looked at call-me-Gavin. "Why do you think she chose that particular method?"

A glint appeared in his eye, but was instantly extinguished in favour of the sad, bloodhound look. "Stand to reason, doesn't it? I mean, her mother. Poor kid. Just couldn't get her mother's suicide out of her brain. Only happened a couple of years ago, so it's still pretty fresh for her. We tried to help, goodness knows, but those claws!"

He gave me a conspiratorial grin. I didn't respond. "How exactly did her mother die?"

He opened his eyes wide, as though surprised that I didn't know. "Overdose, or poison or something. Took something by mouth, anyway. She was dead by the time young Cherry got home from school. History repeating itself."

"Poor Cherry," the rector said. "We should all pray for her."

Terrified that he might want to pray there and then, I leapt up, glancing at my watch. "Goodness, is that the time? I must go. People to see, things to do. Nice to have met you, although not under these circumstances. Please excuse me. 'Bye."

I returned to the station via the Poynter's house, where I picked up Mandy and Jimmy to take them for a nice ride in the police car. They didn't seem to mind, although Mabel was less than impressed.

"They need a responsible adult with them," she warned.

"I know that, thank you Mrs Poynter. I'll make sure they have all the necessary supervision, and I'll personally return them unharmed."

"She seems very concerned about you," I remarked to the kids as I drove them to the station, but this elicited only a grunt in reply.

They opened up when they were settled in the interview room with a coke, a packet of crisps and a chocolate bar apiece. They seemed quite excited about the prospect of being interviewed by the police, which was a welcome change from the usual surly attitude I've come to expect from teenagers I've picked up.

Cherry had been with them in the Poynter household for about eighteen months. They didn't know where she'd been before that, but she had filled Mandy's head with tales of a life of glamour and excitement on the city streets, and she'd had plenty of money.

"But it all went," Jimmy whispered, his eyes alive with excitement. "She was in a right temper about that, but she wouldn't tell us what happened to it. We reckon Mabel and Gavin took it for safe keeping. They used to do that. We're never allowed too much at any one time."

Mandy took up the tale. "Cherry went missing for the first time after that, but they found her and brought her back. She wouldn't speak to any of us for days. The next time, she ended up in court. That's when she was put on probation and the judge said if she did anything else, she'd be sent to a young offenders' institution."

"That's a prison," Jimmy clarified for me.

At that moment the door opened, and a young constable handed me an envelope. It contained another, sealed envelope and a piece of paper. The outside of the sealed envelope read, 'Open only when case solved', and the piece of paper had just one word written on it, 'semen'. I rolled my eyes. Jack does so love his little party tricks. I had no doubt the sealed envelope would contain a name, but would it contain the name that was swinging around in my brain?

I turned my attention back to the youngsters. "How long have you two been with the Poynters?"

Again that surreptitious glance at each other. "Since we were small. Before we started school. We haven't been anywhere else."

"And you like it there?"

Two heads nodded simultaneously, but I had the distinct impression they were hiding something. Never mind. By now I was pretty sure I knew what had happened to Cherry Pye. I ended the interview and drove them home.

Then I made an arrest.

It was late by the time I reached home. The light was on, and the best pathologist in the business was in the kitchen, cooking. I quashed the image of him with a basin of stomach contents, and turned my attention to an excellent meal of carbonara (from a packet), frozen peas, and white wine.

Then, with an air of triumph, I handed him a sealed envelope and held his envelope aloft.

"One, two, three!"

We tore into them in feverish haste. Surprise, surprise, the same name was in each envelope.

"Ladies first," he said.

"Well, I was suspicious right from the start. Her grief seemed a little out of whack, if you know what I mean. Then when I met him, he knew all about my visit, even though I'd asked her not to contact him. More to the point, he knew how Cherry had died. I hadn't mentioned that. When I spoke to the youngsters, they seemed to be quite open, but I knew they were hiding something. That's the only home they know, and I got the impression Cherry was something of a misfit. And the whole family talked too much about Cherry being on the streets. So what I think is this. Call-me-Gavin likes teenage girls, but he's gross—old and fat. I think Cherry went to Mabel, perhaps to blackmail Mabel into handing her money back. Mabel was furious with Gavin, but even more furious with Cherry for 'seducing' him. That was the reason for the emphasis on Cherry being a tom. Mabel forced Cherry to drink an infusion of yew tea, telling her it was good for her and knowing she'd stagger over to the churchyard to be near her mum. Perfect for the tie-up with her mother's suicide."

"Your turn now, clever clogs. How did you work it out?"

He grinned at me in that annoying way he has. "Three things—nearest and dearest, semen, poison being a woman's weapon." He spread his hands. "Simple when you know how, my dear DCI. The question is, now you've arrested Mabel Poynter, is there any way we could fill in the spare time you have?"

It was my turn to grin. "You're the best pathologist in the business, Jack m'lad. Can't you work it out?"

10 SURPRISE!

I dropped in on Jack at lunchtime.

He may be the best pathologist in the business, but to see him eating his sandwiches off a steel gurney right in front of a recently deceased and already decomposing human body, turned my stomach. He offered me a slightly squashed tomato. I shuddered.

He said, "Surprise tonight, Detective Chief Inspector?" with that quirky lift of the eyebrows which always turns me on.

I couldn't help grinning. I knew the code. It meant bed, but I'm not averse to the odd moment of rumpy-pumpy with my husband. "I'll make sure I'm home!"

I skipped off work half an hour early and raced home. I enjoyed a leisurely soak in scented bath water before dressing in that frothy, black lace negligee affair he bought me for Christmas but which I've never worn. Might as well make it an evening to remember.

Then I draped myself casually on the sofa. I'd give him surprise!

I didn't have long to wait. Within fifteen minutes I heard his key in the door, and plastered on my most alluring smile.

For once I really had surprised him. He stood in the doorway gazing at me with a goofy grin on his face. Then he said, "Surprise!" and flung the door wide.

Suddenly the room was awash with a sea of faces. They all crowded in from the department; my constables, sergeants, and even my two detective inspectors. I gasped in horror and snatched up the throw from the sofa, hurriedly wrapping myself in it, but not before a dozen camera phones had flashed at me.

Averting my crimson face, I put on my iciest detective chief inspector voice. It wasn't difficult. "If I see a single picture on Facebook, You Tube, or any other internet site, on any computer, in print, or anywhere else, I will personally break both your legs and stamp on your battered and bruised torso. Do I make myself clear?"

There were nods and mutters of, "Yes, Ma'am," but I spotted the grins and the glances they exchanged as I did my best to sweep out in a dignified manner—which wasn't easy in a black lace negligee with half a mile of sofa throw attached. As I went, I subjected that renegade Jack to my most ferocious glare.

I threw on a pair of jeans and a T-shirt and braved the lounge again. Someone thrust a glass into my hand and they all launched into a tuneless rendition of Happy Birthday.

They'd all brought presents and cards, so I could do no other than accept graciously. They said how marvellous it was of Jack to arrange a surprise party for my birthday. I smiled and nodded and fumed.

Just wait until I get him alone.

My birthday is not until next month.

11 SERENDIPITY BY DESIGN

I caught it quite by chance. I was idly channel-flicking in the hotel bedroom, trying to decide whether to go down for a drink in the bar before dinner. Not (as you know) that I had any objections to a glass or two, but I did occasionally value my privacy. The paparazzi were hugely useful in keeping my profile current, but sometimes they could be intrusive. I wasn't feeling much like intrusion at that particular time. On the other hand, neither was I feeling much like drinking alone in an impersonal hotel room, no matter how glamorous that room might be.

The programme made my decision for me. There it was, on BBC 2's 'Restoration Village', Pennoyer's School at Pulham St Mary. I could hardly believe my eyes. I was immediately transported back to the end desk of the middle row, a thin, anxious child with long, straggly hair, constantly worried about getting into trouble. That school mistress – what was her name? – with the sharp, malicious eyes, peering intently for any sign of weakness so that she could pounce. I lost count of the number of times I was hauled out to the front of the class to have my awful hair dragged back into a rubber band. I swear she kept a selection in her desk just for me. She never picked on Maud Camber, but then, Maud had gorgeous blond hair and more importantly, wealthy parents. At least, that's how it seemed to me then. Now, of course, I realise that the Cambers were only a notch or so above us, but at the time Maud's family was the most alluring group of people I'd ever seen.

I missed most of the television programme with my descent into instant-reverie-land, but I did catch the advert for a road show in the village on the Sunday. I was on my mobile in seconds, making arrangements to travel to Norfolk. I couldn't help it. Something was dragging me back to Pulham St Mary, something from my roots, from the childhood I thought I'd left behind for good. Of course, I had to cover my tracks to avoid the paparazzi, but I'd grown skilled at that over the years. I had outfits from charity shops to suit every occasion and with a pair of dark glasses and a headscarf, I was pretty sure nobody would clock me. Anyway, who would associate little Izzy Webber from the farm worker's cottage with the great Isobella Hyde, star of stage and screen? Nobody, and I mean nobody, knew about my origins and I wasn't about to allow that to change.

It was a shock, reaching the village again after so many years. I parked by the green in Pulham Market and walked the last mile in case I was spotted. Just as well I did, for the village was heaving. There were people everywhere in their shorts and T-shirts and sun tops. I hadn't expected that. Somehow, even though I knew it was a road show, I'd expected Pulham St Mary to be practically empty; the slow, sleepy village I remembered where everything occurred at half speed.

I pushed my way into the school yard and received my second shock, for the school was boarded up and even from the outside, looked to be tottering into oblivion. There was plenty going on in the school yard, with plasterers and wood turners and stone masons all plying their various trades and a stall making and selling straw hats just inside the gates. I thought that was a neat move, for I had vague memories of something about a 'Guild of Hatters', associated with the Guild Chapel which formed the major part of the school. Apparently the Guild Chapel was the interesting element which had ensured a place on the TV programme. The rest was the usual redbrick Victorian monstrosity built in the late eighteen hundreds, although I was amused to see that the loos had been moved inside since my time. Pity, really. The outside loos had been an escape route for me on more than one occasion.

By now I was prepared for the throng of people inside the school, all oohing and aahing over the farsightedness of that old Puritan, William Pennoyer, who had endowed the Guild Chapel as a free school back in the sixteen hundreds. Personally I can't imagine how the Guild Chapel had been his to endow in the first place, since it had stood there since 1401. I suppose he was simply such a wealthy merchant that he was able to buy it. But what really took me by surprise were the school reunions going on all over the place.

'Hetty, darling! Haven't seen you for twenty years!'

'Blast me, Bill Knights! Well, I'm damned! You haven't changed a scrap!' (That must have been a stretch, he looked nearly as old as me.)

'Mrs Taylor! You were my first teacher. How I loved school with you there. You really set me on my way.' (Lucky her. Obviously things improved over the years.)

I didn't see anyone I recognised, which wasn't surprising since we all left at the age of eleven and that was fifty years ago, but I felt a bit deflated, nonetheless. It was as though I was back home, but the house was somehow vacant for me. I don't know quite what I was expecting, but a wave of nostalgia swept over me when I read some of the comments on the graffiti board. School hadn't been brilliant for me, but it had been solid and dependable and I'd felt safe there. Somebody had remembered the old lady who used to live next door, handing us mugs of cocoa over the wall, and in a flash I was back in the fifties, shivering in the school yard but warming my hands on that cocoa.

When unwelcome tears threatened to choke me I made a hasty exit from the school and wandered over to the church, noting en route that The Grange was open with stalls and sideshows and more importantly, Pimms. That mapped out the remainder of my day rather well. Naturally I had never been inside The Grange, for in my day it was a mansion with servants and huge grounds. It was still a mansion with huge grounds, but nobody had servants any more and clearly the present owners were much more approachable than the squire had been. I remember having to curtsey every time his car drove past the school. It was the only car in the village and I guarantee it was a Rolls.

I had a funny feeling when I reached the church. I remembered it as this massive, awe-inspiring building where we had to sit in silence and never move a muscle. Today, I was greeted with a notice which said, 'Thieves beware! You will be caught' and a picture of a CCTV camera underneath. I felt a little sick. That safe feeling began to wobble precariously with this stark reminder of real life. I wandered in, an anonymous pilgrim among many other anonymous pilgrims, and stood gazing sadly at the green mould, evidence of water damage on the wall just inside the door. I plinked a couple of pound coins into the glass jar to ease my conscience, then meandered around the old photos. To my consternation, there were several that featured me between the ages of five and eleven. They were less than flattering and I drew up my collar a little higher. Life would not be worth living if the Press got hold of any of those pictures.

It rocked me a bit to discover that even the church had changed. If the church changes, what can you rely on in these days when life is so often a succession of rapid, quick-fire lurches from crisis to crisis? It seemed to me that the old, austere atmosphere that I recalled so well had gone. The smell of musty hymnbooks had been replaced by the scent of flowers and there was even a Children's Corner complete with books and toys. And on the altar in the Ladychapel was a model maypole with ribbons and pipe-cleaner figures, inviting visitors to join the dance by writing a prayer and laying it on the altar. For a moment I was tempted. There had been something familiar and strengthening about that old rhythm of Day School and Sunday School, no matter how much I complained at the time. But I'd moved well away from any notion of God and besides, why would God want to do anything to help me? Despite my luxury life-style, I knew I'd messed up my life. I'd lost contact with Robert and Catriona, the only people who had ever really loved me. No wonder Catriona had chosen Robert when we divorced. Who would want to live with a mother who was practically alcoholic and whose raison d'etre was to stay young at any cost? Anyway, that was years ago. Why in God's name was I getting so maudlin now?

But I found myself slipping into a pew, well away from the small crowd gathered around the video of the Pulham Pigs airships. Thankfully people were too engrossed in ancient footage of the war and Pulham St Mary's place in it to take any notice of me. I felt the warm wetness of tears on my cheeks before I realised I was weeping, but once I became aware of them, the tears refused to stop. I sobbed and sobbed, as silently as I could, wondering what on earth it was all about and wondering whether I would ever cease crying.

It must have been fully five minutes before I became aware that someone was sitting beside me. She offered me a clean, white handkerchief as I scrabbled for a tissue and I heard myself sniff noisily as I took it.

Then she said quietly in a broad Norfolk accent, 'Izzy Webber. I thought you might show up.'

My heart jumped and my jaw must have dropped as I gaped at her in astonishment. 'Who -? How do you - ? How did you find out who I am?'

She was quite pretty in an elderly, matronly sort of way. Plump of course, but looking comfortable with it; white hair set in curls which fringed her strong face rather attractively.

She laughed, a rich, melodious, genuine laugh. 'I've followed your career from the day you made your first stage appearance. Did you think I wouldn't? I know all about you, Izzy, and I knew you'd come home one day.'

I recognised her, then. 'Maud Camber, as I live and die! You still live here?'

I was certain she detected the slight sneer in my voice, but she was unmoved. She gazed at me with clear eyes which were almost as blue as they had been all those years ago, and I saw only love and kindness in their depths. She said, 'Come back. Come back home to live. Come back where you'll be enclosed within a village which has always loved you. Leave your terrible, destructive life behind. Come back and absorb the healing peace of this place.'

And suddenly I saw my frantic efforts to retain my youth and beauty for the tawdry things they were. I looked at her, so serene and deeply happy and instantly knew that I'd been chasing a rainbow all these years. Deep inside myself I knew that money and fame were immaterial beside the love and healing this place could offer me.

I acted on impulse. I came home. I stayed. I'm really, deeply, properly happy for the first time in years. Oh, and I bought The Grange.

12 A LOVELY BOY

He's a lovely boy, my son. Very concerned about me, caring. Why, he gave me this computer. It arrived by carrier one day. I had to sign for it on a little machine. I didn't make a very good fist of it, but the man didn't worry.

"That's O.K., love."

He whistled as he hopped back into his van and roared off. Of course, he was busy. Had a lot of deliveries that day, I shouldn't wonder.

My computer is called a 'laptop'. It had quite a thick booklet with it and I thought it would take me a long time to get through it the print being so small, but it turned out that only five pages were in English. I looked through all the other languages, Russian, Italian, French, German, Japanese, Saudi Arabian, but they were all Greek to me. (See? As my son says, I haven't lost my sense of humour.) I wasn't sure what to do then, so I just looked at my computer that first day. But I soon had a plan.

Next day I was up really early, standing by the door. I called out to the paper boy as he flew past on his bicycle. He screeched to a halt, flung his bike down and came running over.

"You alright, Missus?"

"Do you know about computers?"

"Computers? 'Course. What about 'em?"

"I have one." I enjoyed the disbelief written all over his face. It's a long time since I've made anyone look like that. "I need a little help. Could you come back after school? I'll pay you."

"How much?"

"Five pounds?"

"That'll get you fifteen minutes. Better make it twenty."

Twenty pounds! But I nodded anyway. I've always been a quick learner, so I considered the money a good investment.

In the end he came back five times, which meant I had to make do with the food already in the pantry for several weeks. But I've lived through a war. I know how to make food stretch. And by the end of the five visits I could not only switch on my laptop, but also play Solitaire, email, and surf the net (see, I even have the lingo). He set me up with an email account and a presence on Facebook and showed me how to do 'instant messaging'.

I must have made many friends around the world, for I get lots of emails every day and some of them are in foreign languages. Some aren't very nice. A lot of people seem to think I want to enlarge my penis, but I don't have one. I kept replying and telling them, but they still wrote. Now, I've stopped replying to those. If I press a little button labelled 'Del', they just disappear so I don't worry too much. It takes me a long time every day to respond to my emails, but people keep sending them even when I don't reply, so it doesn't seem to matter if I miss out on one or two. Some are quite sad. I receive quite a number from a poor African lady whose children are in an orphanage. I try to help her, when I can.

The best thing is, I can talk to my grandchildren now. They were so surprised to see I was on Facebook that now lots of their friends have become my friends too and they send little messages about what they're doing. I like that, although I don't always understand what they mean. I've even emailed my son, to thank him for the computer.

He's a lovely boy. He says he might get to see me soon. But he's very busy, what with work and the house and the family. A mile is a long way when you're so busy. But he's so pleased that I've learned to play Solitaire on my computer and he says I can always email him, whenever I want, so I'll never be lonely again. He's such a lovely boy. So very concerned and caring.

13 FOR GOD'S SAKE

The morning is cold and dark, but I am unhurried. One should not hurry for church but utilise the time to prepare one's soul. Or so I was always taught and so I have endeavoured to practise from my childhood onwards. Of course, these days no-one else bothers, not even the handful of elderly parishioners who attend the eight a.m. service at St. Saviour's. But that does not prevent me from following my duty.

I have a strip wash as it's Sunday and dress carefully in my thick, tweed suit and my sheepskin ankle boots. I wear a woollen muffler - a Christmas gift from dear Rupert in nineteen eighty-six, the last gift I ever received from my brother - and a respectable hat. Not one of those dreadful woolly pompoms that are so popular these days, but my purple felt with the feather. Felt is one of the warmest fabrics as I tell my fellow parishioners, but needless to say, they fail to listen.

It's strange, the way people humour me. They think I don't notice, but I do. After a lifetime of teaching eager young minds, some of whom absorbed knowledge like the proverbial sponge and others into whom I made sure I instilled facts by one means or another, I find it deeply offensive when people turn away with that slight nod and the patronising smile as though I'm nothing but a stupid old woman. Old I may be, but I have never been stupid.

I take my normal place in the fourth pew from the front at my self-appointed time of ten to eight. Naturally I am first, as I like to use those ten minutes to good advantage on my knees in prayerful communion with my Lord.

The Colonel will be next, stomping and harrumphing fit to wake the dead, then little Jane Manders. Plain Jane from Peckham, my mother always used to say. But that was over seventy years ago, when Jane and I were girls together in the Sunday School. She was Jane Didscombe then. She married that idiot Manders when she was barely twenty-one. Fortunately he had the good sense to die and leave her in peace after twenty years of marriage. But she was always a silly, giggly girl and she grew into a twittering woman, like a little bright-eyed bird and with about as much sense.

She slips into the pew next to me, as though we're bosom pals.

"Good morning, Millicent. Cold today, isn't it?" She leans towards me and rubs her hands together unnecessarily to emphasise her point. "I'll be glad when Spring comes."

I incline my head towards her but avert my eyes, wishing she'd sit elsewhere. With half a dozen people in an empty church, she could have had ten pews to herself. But no. She has to sit with me. I should have remained on my knees. That would have forestalled the weekly inanity.

The other three slide into their pews just as the church clock strikes the hour. It is disgraceful, the way people rush in at the last minute, all hot and breathless. Not only does it disturb those of us who are proper worshippers, but it prevents them savouring the full experience of God's peace at this quiet hour. Punctuality is next to godliness, my mother always used to say.

The final member of our little band is Douglas Fern, the churchwarden. At this eight o'clock service he's churchwarden, verger, sidesman and sacristan all rolled into one, although at the ten o'clock service where there will be around thirty worshippers, I believe he is merely churchwarden. I've never attended that service, myself. I prefer traditional worship.

Douglas is the local farmer-cum-landowner and regards himself as the village squire. His family have been churchwardens at St. Saviour's for generations, passed down from father to eldest son. Fortunately Douglas is a bachelor, so the line stops with him. He loves to be at the centre, does Douglas. He's Chairman of the Parish Council (I stubbornly refuse to use this ridiculous political correctness of 'Chair') and of the Board of Governors at the local Church of England Primary School. Oh yes, our Douglas is at the centre of power in this Norfolk village.

It has led to some tensions between him and the Rector, tensions which seem to me to be increasing although naturally, nothing is said. But I see the Rector's lips set in a thin line when he spies Douglas approaching and he has been known to abruptly about turn and disappear into the vestry rather than face Douglas.

Although I have yet to witness one myself, village gossip reports slanging matches between the Rector and his churchwarden. Not that I listen to gossip, but this did come from a reliable source and is common knowledge in the village so I'm not breaking any confidences. Apparently there was a dreadful incident one Sunday, when the Rector arrived for the evening service only to discover that the indelible ink they use for signing the marriage registers had been poured all down the Rector's surplice. Not just any old surplice either, but the lace cotta with the square neck of which the Rector is so proud. I must say he always looked very fine in that cotta. With his height and his very attractive thick, silver hair he can carry it off, especially as he normally has that air of aloofness which is so important in clergy. No question of aloofness on this occasion, though. He was heard to accuse Douglas since only he and Douglas have keys to the vestry. Douglas, unused to having his integrity impeached, retorted furiously that James had probably done it himself to draw attention to himself and to falsely incriminate Douglas.

But why would the Rector want to incriminate Douglas, without good reason?

'No smoke without fire,' the village muttered.

While I don't hold to such clichés myself, it did make me wonder whether perhaps there was some history between the two of them. Both single men of roughly similar age, you'd have thought they would get on well together. And Douglas seemed so thrilled when the Rector came, three years ago. Never before had I seen such a look of eager anticipation on his face. But things have deteriorated sadly since then. I have also heard that whole bottles of Communion wine have gone missing, but I dismiss those rumours with contempt. Douglas drinks in 'The King's Head'. Why would he need Communion wine?

The Rector has started the service and I give myself up to his sonorous tones repeating the old, well-loved words, so familiar from my childhood that I could lead the service myself from memory. Not that I ever would. That place at the altar, standing between the congregation and God, is a man's place as I tell anyone who will listen, especially those poor, misguided fools who hanker after appointing a female curate.

"Never!" I declare robustly. "Over my dead body." And I see them exchange knowing glances as though they're saying, 'That can be arranged.'

But such thoughts are not suitable at the moment. I concentrate on the service with the full focus of my mind. I lose myself in the beauty of the Elizabethan language. I allow the peace of God which passes all understanding to flood into my heart and fill my being.

The service is over all too soon. This brief half-hour on a Sunday morning, the highlight of my week, seems to flash past ever more quickly. I sit for a moment savouring the atmosphere and unwilling to give it up quite so soon. Out of the corner of my eye I see Jane Manders about to engage me in conversation so I shut my eyes very deliberately. She gets the message and scurries off.

I myself am about to leave reluctantly when Douglas Fern rushes past me as though St. Saviour's is on fire. I remain seated. If there is a problem, perhaps I can be of assistance. I don't know whether he even notices me, such is his agitation.

He slams into the vestry and voices are raised.

"I knew it was you! Caught you red-handed. What have you to say for yourself now, I'd like to know?"

"What on earth are you talking about, Douglas? I always count the collection, as you very well know."

"With your hand in last week's bag?"

"Don't be so stupid, man. I'm - I'm checking last week's collection to see - er - to see whether the amount has increased since my appeal for more money."

"And you think the police are going to believe that?"

Never before have I heard Douglas sneer. It is an ugly sound. But not as ugly as the Rector's hissed response.

"The police? Are you completely mad? You think they'll believe your word against mine after all that's gone before?"

I think Douglas is about to explode and I wonder whether I should reveal my presence and intervene. His voice rises several notches until he is nearly screaming.

"You filthy, lying shit! I'll - "

There is a tremendous crash accompanied by a scream which cuts off abruptly. I peer gingerly around the vestry door. Douglas is lying motionless on the floor, blood streaming from a large gash on his head, his sightless eyes turned towards heaven. The Rector is deathly white, his hands shaking. He fails to notice me until I speak.

"Will you be needing a new churchwarden, Rector? I will happily offer myself for the post. As you know, I wish only to serve."

"What?" His eyes are glassy. The sweat pours down his face. "Get out of here, you sanctimonious old bitch!"

He makes towards me somewhat violently, so I remove myself from his presence. Of course, I am aware that it's only the shock talking. And there's plenty of time now, anyway.

I hurry home and alert the police and ambulance services, as duty demands.

The following Sunday, everyone is cloyingly solicitous towards the Rector. So sad about poor Douglas, to trip and fall like that and with the Rector witnessing it all. They crowd around the Rector, cooing and burbling until I have to clear them away. As acting churchwarden until my position can be ratified at the Annual Parochial Church Meeting, I have a duty to protect my Rector.

We get on extremely well, because we understand each other. And I'm so very pleased to see him wearing the Rolex. It's amazing what you can do with a little extra money. After a glass or two of Communion wine, of course.

14 SUNDAY TERROR

It happened on a Sunday morning.

In the past, we've both enjoyed walking, James and me. On days off, we'd take the car to a country area, do a circular walk of some five or six miles, then finish up with lunch at a handy pub. But just lately we haven't been able to do that. James is on tablets which make him breathless, with the result that he now walks like a snail and can manage about ten yards—I exaggerate only slightly.

Walking so slowly makes my back ache—plus my hips, my legs, and my soul—so we've reached an arrangement which has proven satisfactory for both of us. When we motor to the supermarket, James lets me out about a mile or so from home. I stride out the remaining distance, while James drives home, unpacks the car, puts away the shopping, and sets the coffee going. Very acceptable. I like it, anyway.

On Sundays, I set off for church about forty-five minutes before the service is due to start, walking along the narrow country lane to the tiny village church perched on the hill. James leaves half an hour later, and drives up. We generally arrive at church at around the same time, and either meet up at the lych gate or go inside and meet up in the pews.

On this particular Sunday, I was five minutes late leaving. I hadn't slept well, and you know what it's like. You lie there for hours tossing and turning, then fall into a deep sleep about an hour before you're due to get up. When we awoke, James and me, I had only half an hour to shower, dress, and eat breakfast. I didn't make it, hence my late departure.

As I strode up the lane, being that much later I was passed by rather more church-going cars than usual, which meant I had to keep stopping as

I pressed myself into the hedge. It was either that or losing my toes. I generally choose to retain my toes.

I kept expecting James to pass me, but he didn't. Perhaps he'd gone round the other way; he did that occasionally. He wasn't waiting at the lych gate, and when I wandered into church, he wasn't in the pews, either. I felt a little concerned, but not very, since it was still five minutes until the service started.

Every time the great oak door clattered open I turned, but no James. By now I was growing seriously worried. Had he had an accident in the car? Was he lying in a ditch somewhere? Had he passed out with a TIA (transient ischaemic attack—he did that sometimes, hence the tablets) or suffered a heart attack?

Needless to say, this was the one Sunday when I'd forgotten to bring my mobile phone with me.

I'd have walked out of church then and there to look for him, but for the fact that I was due to lead the intercessions. I'd have to stick it out, but the worry was mounting. I was unable to concentrate on the service, but found myself praying over and over again, "Please God, let him be all right."

The service seemed interminable, although in truth it was no more than the usual hour. I rushed out the minute it was over, not waiting to exchange any pleasantries or shake any hands, and practically ran home, looking out all the while for dead bodies in ditches.

I was completely breathless myself by the time I reached home. I opened the front door with dread, my heart full of fear. What would I find?

I found my husband sitting in front of the Open Golf competition on television, his feet up, the Sunday paper by his elbow and a glass of beer in his hand.

I leave you to imagine the conversation between James and me. Say what you like, feel free. I did.

15 MORE SUNDAY TERROR

It was a normal enough Sunday. I bustled around making tea and toast and getting myself ready for church, while Patrick lounged in the conservatory reading the Sunday papers. He pops along to the local shop at nine o'clock every Sunday morning, returning with an armful of Sunday papers, all complete with their magazine sections. Don't know what he sees in them, myself. To me, all Sunday papers are alike. When you've skimmed through one, you've skimmed the lot. Still, it keeps Patrick happy for the whole of Sunday, so I shouldn't grumble.

We've been married for twenty-four years, ten months and two weeks, Patrick and I. I'm Sarah, by the way. Was Sarah Coppice until Patrick Nicholson spotted me across a crowded office party twenty-five and a half years ago. The rest, as they say, is history.

I'm SO looking forward to our twenty-fifth wedding anniversary—and no, he isn't buying me anything silver. He did offer (with the requisite quantity of arm-twisting,) but what I've always wanted is to travel to New Zealand to visit my brother and his family. I've never seen his wife or his grown-up children, only in photos. He went there twenty years ago, married a New Zealand girl, and has never been back since, so you can see how important it is to me to get in one visit. Patrick agreed. He's never been much for travelling (can barely get him to shift from the conservatory and certainly not out of Norfolk) but he promised to buy tickets for our silver anniversary.

I've spent the last few months getting ready for the trip, even though it's still six weeks away. Well, you have to have a new wardrobe, don't you? Can't travel all that way without the latest fashions. I've bought new stuff for Patrick too, but he doesn't seem to take much notice. The shirts are still in their cellophane wrappings, and he didn't even bother to try on the new trousers.

I hummed happily as I strolled back from church. It had been a good service and I felt uplifted. God was in his heaven and all was right with the world.

I called out to Patrick as I came through the door, but he didn't answer. No surprises there, then. Once he was engrossed in his newspapers, nothing penetrated his consciousness. I wandered through to the conservatory—but he wasn't there. Now that was a surprise. He's usually glued to his seat (apart from the obvious necessary excursions from time to time) for the whole day.

He wasn't in the lounge either, nor the kitchen, the bedrooms, the bathroom, or the garage. Neither was he in the garden. Patrick had vanished.

I didn't worry for the first hour. After all, he was a grown man, he could do as he pleased. So what if he'd taken it into his head to go out for a stroll?

By the second hour I was growing rather more nervous, and by the third, I was distinctly tetchy. What on earth was he playing at? And what should I do about supper?

To distract myself from anxious thoughts, I got out my knitting and sat down in front of the television. I was knitting a nice sweater in rainbow colours for Patrick. Those New Zealand nights might be cold.

It was when I glanced at the clock that I became aware of a sheet of paper thrust behind it. Throwing down my knitting, I fished out the paper and straightened it. Torn from a notebook, it said in Patrick's poor excuse for handwriting, 'Gone to—something I couldn't read—Aimee. Sorry it's so near the NZ trip, but hope you understand. P.'

What on earth? Oh my God! Did this mean what I thought it meant? Surely not! I mean, I know he's been a bit distant lately, but another woman! And just before our trip, too.

For a moment I stood there like a goldfish, with my mouth open and about the same ability to concentrate. Then I sat down heavily. Who was Aimee, and more to the point, what was I going to do?

How could he do this to me? How could he leave me like this after twenty-five years of marriage, and with just a scribbled note? I know we have no family, but that was hardly my fault. He was the one with the low sperm count, although I've tried hard not to blame him. He was the one who refused to adopt, too. Said he wasn't taking on other people's genetic problems. What rubbish! This wouldn't have happened if we'd had a family.

Of course, we had the two dogs, and they were good company. Dear little things, fluffy, gorgeous lapdogs—Poms from the same litter, Jo and Beth—but sad to say, our Poms didn't live very long. They should have lived for fifteen years, but only made ten. Patrick blamed me—me! who loved them like my children—saying I should have fed them dry dog food, not rich scraps from my plate. But who took them out for walks every day, I'd like to know?

But now—now it seemed I was on my own. No dogs, and no Patrick. He'd left me for this trollop from work. She must have been from work, otherwise I'd have known her. Darned if I was going to take it lying down though. I could feel rage building inside me. He'd taken the best years of my life and for what? To leave me utterly alone in my twilight years? We'd soon see about that.

First thing tomorrow I'd take myself off to my solicitor, change the locks—Patrick needn't think he was coming back, ever—and storm into his office where I'd—

I heard the front door open. He sauntered into the lounge grinning, can you believe it? I flew at him, beating on his chest and clawing a long scratch down the side of his face. I was pleased to see I drew blood.

For a moment he was too surprised to react, then he held my arms. "Whoa! Steady on, old girl. Don't you want to meet Aimee?"

"Meet her? Meet your fancy piece? How dare you! How long has this been going on behind my back? If you're thinking of a threesome, you've another think coming! You—you—"

I could feel myself spluttering in my fury, but Patrick just looked at me in that annoyingly calm way he has, and began to laugh. Before I had a chance to spit even more venom, he pulled me to the door and out to the car. There in the boot was the daintiest, cutest, fluffiest, most delightful little Pom puppy you ever could see.

Patrick said, "Meet Aimee. I'm sorry she's come so close to our trip, but I've made sure she's had all her injections so she'll be ready to go back to the same kennels, where they know and love her. That's why I've been so long. The veterinary side took longer than I expected. What do you think?"

What did I think? I thought I had the most wonderful, beautiful, perfect husband who ever walked God's earth. But how I wish I could read his handwriting.

16 YET MORE SUNDAY TERROR

It happened on Sunday, as I was walking home from church.

Over the last twenty or thirty years there have been occasional reports in the media of black panthers roaming the countryside here in Norfolk. Nobody has seen any of these creatures close up and there are no reliable photographs, but nonetheless, the rumours resurface from time to time. The theory is that a pair escaped from captivity (although no zoo or wild life park will admit to losing any) and produced offspring, so there is now thought to be a family living wild and roaming the whole of Norfolk.

Some years ago, my husband swears he saw one, way over across the fields. Since it was early morning and he was half asleep on his way to play golf and there was a low Autumn mist clinging to the fields, I laughed. Probably a big, black Labrador, I told him, and ignored his indignant denials.

On Sunday, the sky was an untroubled blue and the sun was hot on my back, the perfect day for a walk. As I returned from church I noticed a footpath along the edge of a wheat field. The other side of the path was fringed with trees offering welcome shade, and in the distance I could see what I thought was a group of houses nestling together. The footpath was beckoning me, although I had no idea where it led.

"Come this way," it seemed to be calling to me, so I did. It would make me late reaching home, but what the heck? Why be indoors on a day like this?

I wandered onto the footpath following it through the wheat field, but discovered that it went further than I had thought, across an empty meadow. Still, there was civilisation at the other end—or so I thought—in the form of the houses.

I continued on my way. It was quite exciting finding a new walk, but the meadow turned out to be a long one which never seemed to end. The houses remained just as far away as when I started, and the trees to my left thickened until I found I was walking along the edge of a wood.

It was then that I spotted the black panther on the other side of the meadow. It was standing quite still, its head alert and ears pricked, gazing at me. My heart started to hammer. I glanced back the way I'd come. Was it nearer to go back, or to go forward? Needless to say, I was almost exactly half way.

My heart pounding, I decided to go on. Moving as slowly and as cautiously as I could, I prayed the animal was too far away to smell my fear, but as I moved, so did the panther. No black Labrador, this. It was long and rangy, with a small head and pointed, tufted ears, and I had a horrible feeling it regarded me as potential dinner.

I tried standing completely motionless again, but still it crept towards me. When it was close enough for me to observe it quite clearly, it sank to its haunches, ready to spring.

I shifted then like greased lightning, racing towards the houses—which turned out to be not houses at all but a group of derelict farm buildings—as fast as I could. I heard the low growl and the snarl as the panther easily outpaced me, but I thought I might at least manage to hide in the trees.

Even as I thought it, I tripped and fell, sprawling headlong on the ground. With one bound the panther was upon me. Its teeth sank into my trousers and it started pulling my leg.

Just like I'm pulling yours.

17 THE S-C-R-EEEAAM

Despite the warmth of the day and the cloudless blue sky overhead, that blood-curdling scream chilled me to the bone.

I was strolling through shaded woodlands and country meadows full of the most gorgeous wild flowers – poppies, bugle, daisies, scabei, dog roses, ladies' slipper – enjoying the gentle scents and the buzzing of honey bees, the busy, colourful butterflies and iridescent dragonflies, when the peace of the morning was split by a shrill, terrifying scream. Had it been night time I would have suspected a ghost, even though I don't believe in them. Not really. Not in day time, anyway. Ghosts only emerge after dark. Don't they?

The hairs stood up on the back of my neck and my fingertips tingled as adrenaline coursed through my body. Fight or flight? I crouched involuntarily, as though to keep at bay the evil depicted by that unnatural scream. But I was curious. I'm Jane – Jane Parker – known to all and sundry as Nosey Parker, so obviously I was determined to do what I could for that tortured victim. Or at least, to find him or her.

At a light lope, I turned in what I thought was the direction of the scream. Leaving the woodland path I found myself alongside a high brick wall, stretching for miles, enclosing a country estate. As I inched towards large, wrought iron gates, I heard the scream again. Slightly lower pitched this time, it lasted a moment or two longer but was just as chilling. I wondered whether it ended in a sob. My heart began to thump against my chest.

A child being tortured or kidnapped? An adult in pain?

As I glanced up at the forbidding gates to ascertain whether I could access the grounds that way, I was assailed by horrible, high-pitched yapping. Just my luck! A couple of Yorkshire terriers informing the whole world of my presence. You might have thought a place this size would have German Shepherds patrolling, but no, all they needed were these noisy mutts.

Yes, you may look cute with your tails wagging fit to bust, but I know what you'd do, given half a chance. You'd be nipping at my heels and sinking your sharp little teeth into my calf the minute you were out of that gate. Dream on, dogs! I'm not coming in that way.

Anyway, the gates were far too high to scale, and had electronic wizardry together with a very unwelcoming 'Keep Out' notice. I stood for a moment gazing through the gates, up the curving drive towards the house. Well, mansion really. One of those large, modern, red brick affairs pretending to be a manor in extensive grounds, its façade pretentiously embroidered by white stone columns, matching the white stone lions on pillars which guarded the gates.

I stood for only a moment, while the terriers wound themselves into a frenzy of anticipation, then I slunk away, creeping along the wall, hoping to put the dogs off the scent and to find another entry somewhere further round.

Eventually, by the time I'd put half a mile between me and the gates and the dogs had lost interest, the yapping gradually died away. But I could still hear the screeches, as piercing and disturbing and as mind-numbing as ever.

A little farther, and I came upon exactly what I'd been seeking. An old door set in the wall. I turned the handle and pushed, but either it was locked or it hadn't been opened for years. Probably the latter, by the state of the ivy encrusting it.

There was no help for it. I put my shoulder against the door and shoved. It gave a millimetre, but I was encouraged. I crashed into it with my shoulder again and again, until it suddenly realised I meant business, and gave way, hanging drunkenly on its hinges. My arm was hanging drunkenly too, but what the heck! I was in. Now all I had to do was locate the source of that terrible searing cry, and ring the police. Not necessarily in that order, since I admit to an unmistakeable yellow streak.

I pushed my way through waist-high nettles, cursing my sleeveless top and open sandals but gritting my teeth against the stings. I thrust aside brambles which tore at my clothes and my exposed skin and staggered through thorny undergrowth which felt as thick and unforgiving as Sleeping Beauty's enchanted forest.

At last I emerged onto the edge of the manicured lawn and flower beds, facing the patio to the rear of the mansion house. And there I saw them.

Two colourful peacocks proudly strutting their stuff and loudly announcing their beauty as only peacocks can.

18 HALLOWEEN EXPERIENCE

I'd forgotten it was Halloween, hence I had nothing in the house for potential Trick-or-Treaters, a minor disaster since I didn't want to wake in the morning to discover my doorknob covered in treacle. In my experience, these Trick-or-Treaters are only too happy to trick.

I got out the car and raced the ten miles to the nearest supermarket, where I had previously spied large bags of Halloween sweets, specially produced by a well-known confectionery firm. Made out of liquorice or fruit gum, the bag contained witches hats, broomsticks, snakes, black cats, cauldrons, and so on. You get the picture.

It was already late so I might have missed the Trick-or-Treaters already, but if so, I reckoned I could snuggle down in front of the television and happily eat the bagful of goodies myself.

On the way back I had to pass the churchyard, dark and forbidding on this night of all nights. I was about to accelerate past when I heard an ear-splitting screech. Until then, I'd never understood the expression about the hairs on the back of your neck standing up, but now I knew.

As the unearthly scream was repeated, against my better judgement I parked the car, forced myself to get out, and ventured cautiously through the lych gate into the churchyard. There being no lighting whatsoever, and this being the middle of the countryside, it was black as pitch. Needless to say, I had no torch with me, not even in the car. Still, I couldn't stop now. It sounded like someone was being murdered. Either that, or the ghosts of long deceased parishioners really were abroad.

My heart was hammering in my chest and my mouth was dry as I edged forwards towards the cacophony, bruising my shins on gravestones and stumbling over stone monuments to the dead. I found myself clutching the small wooden cross I carry in my pocket, as if to ward off evil.

I moved as quietly as I could, but with no light it was impossible to be silent. For a moment the howls ceased, and I was even more terrified. Had some supernatural presence detected me? Were vampires or demons or spirits about to descend? I held my breath and remained perfectly still, but nothing happened except that the evil screeching started up again.

I followed the noise as best I could, but to my surprise it seemed to lead me out of the churchyard and into the vicarage garden next door. As softly as I could, I clicked open the gate and slipped into the vicarage garden, closer now to that terrible sound.

At that very moment, a light came on in the upstairs bedroom of the vicarage, the window opened, and an angry voice yelled, "Stop that bloody noise!"

The next moment I was drenched in a bucket of cold water, and two cats fled.

I slunk home as quickly as I could, changed into dry gear and spent the rest of the evening snuggled in front of the television, grazing on Halloween goodies. I didn't go to church next day.

19 THE DEVIL OF A TIME

Okay, so I was late leaving, but it wasn't my fault. Honestly.

I dressed to kill in a pencil slim skirt that hugged my slender hips, and a matching jacket in apple green, plus a pale green shirt open at the collar with a couple of buttons strategically undone, giving a generous but tantalising view of the rosy top of my breasts.

Of course I should have fed the cat first. I know that now, there's no need to tell me. But I didn't know it then, and when Her Ladyship Queen Cam sensed food was imminent, she leaped at me, dragging her claws down my skirt and scraping through my tights.

I leave you to imagine the result.

So by the time I'd screamed at the cat, changed into the only other suit I possess (in a sad shade of donkey brown), and tugged at my blonde curls which refused to straighten so tied them back in what turned out to be an Afro pony tail, I was twenty minutes late leaving.

Sod's Law being what it is, I was so held up en route, arriving in a lather of unseemly sweat (naturally it was the hottest day of the year, and this was a very hot venue), completely breathless and unbelievably dishevelled.

"Come in and sit down, Miss De'Ath," the main one said, in tones that would cut the heart from a block of ice. Each of them glanced ostentatiously at their watches, then glared at me with cold, blank eyes. The 'dress to kill' look was having no effect whatsoever. I might as well have worn jeans. Might have been on time if I had.

The only female in the line up of five males seated rigidly behind the marble table said coldly, "We assume you have an explanation for your tardiness, Miss De'Ath?" No fellow feminine feeling there. Her gaze was relentless, boring through my very soul.

Oh well. Probably lost the job long before I arrived, so might as well make the most of it. Nothing to lose.

I sat back in my chair and took a deep breath. I decided to tell them everything – apart from the incident with the cat, obviously.

"I've had such a terrible journey getting here. The traffic jam was four miles long; it took twenty minutes to get through it. Then, just as we were all getting going again, a deer shot across the road, crashed into the lead car which toppled over the bank down into the river. All four doors jammed, so all four occupants were drowned. Meanwhile the deer veered into the second car, which swerved into the third. That caused a domino effect, with six cars piling into each other. A lorry at the back jack-knifed and slewed across the road, causing four cars on the other carriageway to crash into each other. The road was completely blocked in all directions, so none of the emergency vehicles could get through. There were another three deaths, two critical injuries, and six more taken to hospital.

"As you can see, it took hours. Utter mayhem. That's why I'm late."

I sat back smiling expectantly, but from the scowls and glares it was clear none of them believed a word I'd said. They looked at each other, muttering together behind closed hands, occasionally shooting me a venomous glance. I couldn't hear a word they were saying.

Then the main one cleared his throat. "I'm afraid we don't find you convincing, Miss De'Ath."

"So – do I get the job?"

Suddenly he beamed. "Of course! You're just what we're looking for – someone who brings a string of death, destruction, mayhem and lies. Welcome to my council."

And as he shot out a scaly hand to grip mine, his horns glowed red and his tail thrashed.

20 FUTURE IMPERFECT

"Do you turn to Christ?"

"I turn to Christ."

"Do you repent of your sins?"

"I repent of my sins."

"Do you renounce evil?"

"I renounce evil"

Alice murmured the familiar responses mechanically, heavy with fatigue and the weight of the sleeping baby in her arms. It was so hot in the tiny church. A lone fly was droning overhead, and Alice wondered fleetingly whether it would land on Jonathan and be baptised with him. She'd be glad when it was all over, and she could escape.

She came to with a start as her father gently removed Jonathan from her arms.

"Jonathan David, I baptise you in the name of the Father, and of the Son, and of the Holy Spirit. Amen."

Alice waited for the screams. Jonathan David had barely emerged from the womb before emitting his first piercing shrieks, and had progressed from strength to strength, mostly in the middle of the night. Maliciously, Alice prayed he'd embarrass her father and the new grandmothers, although she couldn't remember ever having heard a baby cry during her father's baptisms. But for him and the grandmothers, Alice wouldn't be here now. But you can't spend your entire life growing up in a vicarage and not have your first child baptised. Or at least, Alice couldn't.

Was Jonathan going to wail? Perhaps if the new grandparents heard something of Jonathan they'd stop cooing for five minutes and realise their first beloved grandson was a monster. But inevitably, Jonathan chuckled and gurgled as the holy water poured over his head, a picture of innocent baby perfection.

The congregation welcomed Jonathan into the flock with applause. Alice glanced at them cynically. She'd known most of them all her life. The congregation didn't change much in small villages. They were full of smiles and nods now, but none of them would care if they never saw Jonathan or herself again. She had no doubt tongues had surpassed themselves wagging a few months back.

A movement towards the rear of the worshippers caught her eye. Alice stared. Why was that youth here in church at the baptism? Alice couldn't remember ever having seen a more incongruous figure. His hair, which was probably blond although it was difficult to determine, was shaven on one side of his head but hung down in three long, greasy, plaited strands on the other. His clothes, a kind of bomber jacket in some strange silvery material, and denim jeans with odd patches which changed colour every time he moved, added to his bizarre appearance. Alice presumed it was the latest fashion, although she'd never seen anything like it before.

The strange young man caught her gaze, and held it. Alice shivered, despite the heat. His eyes were hard and angry. Alice felt a touch of fear. He was glaring at her with some intensity, as though she had injured him in some way. There was something horribly familiar about him, yet she knew she'd never seen him before. He could hardly be a regular member of the congregation, most of whom were over eighty, so why was he here? Perhaps he was a newcomer to the village, or more likely, an escapee from that remand home in Norwich. Escaped before they got the scissors to that dreadful hair, Alice mused. She resolved to mention him to her father.

Her attention returned to her father, now tracing the sign of the cross in holy oil on the baby's forehead, then stooping to kiss him before handing him back. That was an inspired touch which the elderly ladies of the congregation always loved. Alice sighed. She'd seen the ritual so often before that it held almost no meaning for her. Yet she was aware of a faint sense of loss, of the whisper of a desire to return to those irenic childhood days when faith was taken for granted and nothing had happened to cause her to question the existence of God.

She glanced up again towards the stranger, certain in the depths of her being that he didn't believe in God. But the young man had disappeared, had slipped out unnoticed. The service was nearly over now. Just the christening bash in the church hall to endure, then Alice would be mercifully free to return to her own little cottage. She resolved to withstand all pressure to stay the night at the vicarage. There'd be no bad dreams tonight. She felt so exhausted she was certain she'd fall asleep immediately, if Jonathan let her.

Alice wandered through to the church hall, smiling and nodding to well-wishers, Jonathan held securely in her arms.

Daphne materialised silently at her elbow. "Shall I hold him for you while you get something to eat? I've had mine."

Alice was about to respond, "I'm not hungry, it's too hot to eat." But she recognised the impassioned plea behind her mother-in-law's timid words, and thrust Jonathan at her with a smile. She felt sorry for Daphne. It was bad enough to spend most of your fertile years as a widow, but to lose your only son in a horrific accident was beyond what most people could bear. Alice jerked her thoughts away from Daphne. Thoughts of Daphne were too uncomfortably close to thoughts of David, and she wasn't yet ready to tread those appalling depths of darkness.

She wandered over to the long trestle tables, covered with white sheets and laden with the customary buffet food produced, as ever, by the willing hands of the Mothers' Union. Picking up a limp cardboard plate with its attendant paper serviette, Alice chose at random a few sandwiches, curling now in the heat, and the obligatory sausage roll. She had no intention of eating anything, but a full plate tended to stave off comment.

It was as she reached over for a stick of celery filled with cream cheese that a gaunt, male hand stretched towards her. It was a bony hand with unkempt, grimy fingernails and a huge skull ring on the middle finger and this time Alice was as close to the stranger as breathing, and it frightened her. She could detect a faint sweetish odour about him which she couldn't immediately identify, but which stirred some dim memory below the surface of her mind and made her wrinkle her nose in disgust. Now she could see the pallor of his skin, thrown into sharp relief by the burning intensity of those eyes, the same baby blue as Jonathan's, but which were boring into her as though he would question her very soul.

Alice abruptly spun about. She threaded her way through the guests towards her father, who was dispensing sparkling wine in paper cups. She plucked at her father's sleeve.

"Did you see him, Dad? That chap with the hair?"

Her father frowned and shook his head, concentrating on the task in hand. Alice sighed. "Oh Dad, surely you noticed him? He stands out enough in this lot!"

The vicar raised his head fleetingly and skimmed the room. "Must have gone now, Alice. I'll look out for him, though. Your mother may have spotted him."

As Alice circulated amongst the guests, it became disturbingly apparent that nobody had seen him.

As soon as the speeches were over, Alice made her excuses. It had been a long day, and she was anxious to get to bed, for fatigue was making her feel slightly peculiar. She'd noticed for some time now difficulty in concentration, which she was convinced was due solely to lack of sleep. Perhaps the young stranger had been a mirage, due to the excessive heat and her exhausted condition.

Alice wound down both front windows of the car to induce some circulation of cooler air for herself and Jonathan, and drove slowly through the winding country lanes. She'd only been driving again for a couple of weeks, and still felt very shaky. Had she been living anywhere other than Norfolk, she suspected she might never have braved the wheel again. But five or six months in the village without transport, had forced her to return to the driving seat despite her terrors.

She had stopped at the crossroads, leaning forwards to peer carefully left and right round the overgrown hedgerows, when without warning, a dishevelled head with its caustic eyes thrust through her open window. Alice screamed. The baby woke and began to cry, with loud, rending wails.

"Go away! Get out!" shrieked Alice. She made to push at the head with its strange, greasy hairstyle, but even as she lunged, the head vanished. Alice put her foot down, and the little car shot forward, narrowly missing a holiday-maker travelling at a leisurely pace on the other road. Heart pounding and limbs trembling, Alice didn't dare stop until she reached her own little drive.

She gathered up the baby and ran into the house, slamming and locking the door behind her. She took the baby into bed with her, for company. The trembling hadn't stopped, even after a large gin. Who was that guy, and what did he want with her? And whom did he resemble, despite his bizarre appearance? He had Jonathan's eyes, and – and David's nose! Why, he was a little bit like her dead husband!

Alice shuddered, and closed her eyes. She must have slept, for she awoke feeling cold. She was about to get up and close the window when she became aware of the figure half hidden in shadow. She screamed – hopelessly - for she knew there was no-one within earshot of her tiny cottage.

The young man glared at her, with his angry, accusing eyes.

"Who are you?" whispered Alice. "Are you a ghost? What do you want with me?"

The eyes slowly swung until they focussed on the baby, peacefully sleeping beside her. In a flash, Alice understood. She understood everything with a deep clarity. This wasn't some spectre of David, a ghost of the past. It was an apparition of Jonathan their son, a ghost of the future. This was what Jonathan would be like in nineteen years' time, this awful specimen with the smell of cannabis or some such hanging round him, unrecognisable apart from the eyes. And those eyes, accusing, always accusing her of causing his father's death.

Alice knew what she must do. She hugged her baby tightly to her, and kissed him gently. "I love you so much," she whispered. Then she picked up the pillow and held it firmly over Jonathan's face. And as the writhing limbs slowly stilled and the whimper gradually died away, so the phantom in front of her slowly vanished from her sight.

Alice sighed deeply, and lay down to sleep.

21 ADRENALINE RUSH

18th August 2058. My birthday, and a major one at that.

I feel an unexpected frisson of excitement as I boil a mug of water for caffeine and I catch myself humming in the shower. I've been saving my energy allowance for months for this one trip into Norwich and it's an early start as I need to be about before the Energy Police get abroad, even though my journey is perfectly legal. The Energy Police are recognised as being somewhat over-enthusiastic, but I refuse to buy into the whispered gossip about unexplained disappearances and torture cells. This is rural Norfolk. Things like that don't happen here.

The sky is the usual cloudless blue, with the sun already blazing at this early hour. Although I daren't use the air-con, the house and garage are well insulated and I slip into the car without having to face the heat. I keep my temperature down by wearing my air-con gear, tight black trousers with a fitted black cotton polo sweater, circulating coolness via my own electrical discharges. Black, of course, to counteract the sun. Most of us wear black these days, although I refuse to keep my blonde hair completely covered by a black scarf, defiantly ensuring a few escaping tendrils.

The car is fully charged, sufficient for the thirty-four mile round trip with some to spare. I love this journey into Norwich for it gives me time to gaze at the fields and hedgerows. Must stop myself wallowing in nostalgia, though. I see the kids' eyes glaze over when folk begin to say, "Do you remember when we had cattle in the fields . . . ?"

Youngsters today have never known anything but underground barns for sheep and cows and pigs. I miss the animals myself, but these self-contained units running entirely on animal-produced methane are so technologically efficient, disease-free and cheap, that I don't complain. Today it's just good to be out in the fresh air for once. Or at least, to be out in the reconditioned air inside the car.

The roads are empty, since we ordinary folk mostly travel on public transport these days. I experience a heady feeling of freedom. Foolish I know, since the battery will die after fifty miles and I won't have enough energy points left to repeat this journey for many months. But just for the moment I could skip across the meadows.

There I go again, the sort of sentimental slush which I promised myself I'd avoid. I remind myself forcibly that I wouldn't be able to stagger fifty metres in this heat and fortunately, common sense prevails.

Within half an hour I'm weaving my way along Haymarket and Gentleman's Walk towards Jarrolds, one of the few department stores which refused to succumb to flash flooding. I like to park on the ground floor so that I can do everything under one roof.

My skin is fairly tingling now with anticipation. It's my special day and I just know I'm going to get Karl for my treatment. I bound up the stairs and sink into one of the large, leather armchairs in the waiting room. The music is soft and soothing, the water feature trickles gently over its pebbles, the fragrance elicits the forgotten scent of flowers and I find myself relaxing.

The door opens. It is Karl! Oh my God, he looks better than ever. Surely he's grown an inch since my last visit? And that dusky skin with the square jaw and the penetrating brown eyes . . . My own eyes flick down to his muscular shoulders and well-honed torso. He is indeed a Greek god. They all are, of course, but I prefer Karl's choice of physical characteristics. Not for the first time, I wonder how old he is. He looks about thirty, but so do most men these days.

As I lie on the couch with Karl's strong hands caressing my body, I give up all speculation and surrender myself to pure sensuality. I have no idea how much time is passing or even how Karl is implanting the treatment. I just know how good it feels.

It's over all too soon. As I dress, Karl assesses me with a professional eye. "Younger than ever!" he declares approvingly and I smile with pleasure at the flattery, kidding myself that this time I really do detect a gleam in his eye.

I bumble up to the revolving restaurant on the top floor for lunch. It is pleasantly full and I smile and nod as I'm led to my table. I may know some of these people. Difficult to tell who I know now that we all choose our looks. I feel a twinge of anxiety which is never present during my virtual interactions at home. It feels odd and somewhat threatening to be greeting real people, even though it has to be said that most of the women resemble that familiar antique the Barbie doll, and most of the men resemble Ken.

Lunch is wonderful. Real food, cooked in the old conventional way. Since restaurants like this are partially exempt from energy rationing, it's out with the laser and back to the old-fashioned cooker. I savour every mouthful since I need the memory to remain with me for at least a year. As I eat, I gaze out at the slowly rotating Norwich skyline, seeing the cathedral and the river and the castle and all those dear, familiar landmarks.

Ages ago I booked Lisa for the afternoon's makeover and she doesn't disappoint. I place myself entirely in her hands and let her get on with it. I emerge with a completely new make-over and a mass of curls which I don't much like but which Lisa assures me is in at the moment.

I float on cloud nine as I drive slowly home, my mind a continuing reverie of the day's events. I'm nearly at the Pulham crossroads down the A140, when at the periphery of my vision I spot movement. This is so unusual that I brake for a closer look.

It's a human being, but not a Ken look alike. Immediately I suspect a climate refugee from Yarmouth and I dither. The official advice is never to stop, but ancient memories are stirring at the base of my mind and some long-forgotten moral sense tells me that I cannot leave another human being out in this heat, whatever the risk. I stop. I approach the man cautiously, but it's only as I reach him that I spot the ski mask.

Suddenly the world erupts. I'm surrounded by three other masked men who come from nowhere. They wrench my arms behind my back and I sense the click of handcuffs. My heart is slamming against my ribs. I gulp a lungful of air. My mouth is dry. I begin to shake uncontrollably.

I'm screaming and crying as they thrust a sack over my head. I kick out and screech at them, "Who are you? What do you want? I'm entitled to this journey. How dare you – "

But I'm bundled roughly into the boot of my car and all sound is cut off with the crash of the boot lid.

I'm beginning to wheeze, my breath coming in short, sharp heaves. I can feel my bowels loosening and I hang on grimly, fighting the terror which is threatening to engulf me. I'm sweating fear and whimpering like a kitten.

I have no idea where we travel nor how far. When we stop and they pull me from the boot, I'm completely disorientated. They drag me into a building and shove me into a room. I'm at the point of collapse when they tear the sack from my head.

Blinding flashes from all directions. Raucous laughter. I cringe, dreading what must come.

Suddenly the room is flooded with light. As I cower against the wall, shielding my eyes from the unexpected glare, I gradually become aware that they are all there. All the family.

"Happy Birthday!" they chorus.

71

My son-in-law and three of my grandsons peel off their masks and stand there expectantly with stupid grins on their stupid faces.

"Better than that freefall parachute jump or the hot air balloon, eh Ma?" beams my son-in-law. I long to slap him, but I smile, weakly.

I stumble to the table and manage to show appropriate amazement at the ten identical cakes each with twelve candles, one for every year of my life. I pose for the statutory photograph with my descendants, although you'd be hard pressed to distinguish any one of us from another. We all look identical; the same age, the same features, clones of sameness. I struggle to smile and joke, trying to appear as though I'm thoroughly enjoying myself.

I gaze at faces which have lost all sense of meaning in the desperate pursuit of eternal youth and it's like looking into a mirror. I see my empty, pointless life endlessly stretching ahead of me, enlivened only by increasingly bizarre events to ensure an occasional adrenaline rush.

And I wish – I really, really wish at the age of one hundred and twenty – that it was possible to die.

22 THE LORD WILL PROVIDE

"Come on, let's get to it. We're going to win this one." Sergeant Anderson strode out of the door, with me trotting along behind him.

As it was my first case, I was determined to make a good impression. Besides, Terry Anderson was definitely tasty, from the top of his curly dark head to the tip of his shining shoes. Of course, every woman in the entire department fancied him. He had an enviable reputation as a ladies' man. Enviable, that is, among the male personnel in CID. We women were less happy about his reputation, but somehow or other that only added to his charm. Naturally, I had no intention of falling into his clutches, but that didn't prevent me wanting him to think well of me. I'd been dreaming of this day for years, ever since I first read the Nancy Drew books my grandmother had stashed away in her bookcase, next to her Bible.

"Where do we start, Sarge?"

He sighed, as though it was the most ridiculous question on earth. "With the old lady, of course. You always start with the victim. Didn't they teach you anything at college?"

"Oh, I know that! I meant after the victim. Where do we go then?"

He quirked an eyebrow and slid me a sideways glance as we climbed into the car. He wasn't fooled for a moment.

Old Mrs Bennett was still in shock. Sitting on her worn sofa in her little cottage, she rocked backwards and forwards, moaning softly.

"Saunders, get us some tea, will you?"

I glanced at the old lady. She looked as if she needed some tea, but I was somewhat miffed at being sent out of the room. Besides, I wasn't sure she would want me rooting about in her kitchen.

Terry Anderson said, "Are you waiting for something, Saunders? Get into the kitchen and do as you're told."

I scuttled off with my head down, but inwardly I was seething. I may have been a newbie, but I didn't see why that gave him the right to treat me as a slave. And how was I going to learn anything if I didn't hear what he said to her? I clattered some mugs as pointedly as I could, set the kettle to boil, then placed my ear to the door and peered through the crack.

Terry had sat down next to the old lady, and had taken her hand. He was gazing into her eyes as though she was the only person in the whole world who mattered to him, and he was hanging onto her every word. For her part, old Mrs Bennett was responding to him just as every woman between the ages of nine and ninety has always responded to him. She was returning his gaze with undisguised admiration, and pouring out her heart. Except—what was that? Did he really say that? That can't be right!

I marched in with three mugs of tea, setting them down on the coffee table in the centre of the room. Terry helped himself to two heaped spoonfuls of sugar. I sent a meaningful glance in his direction, but he failed to notice it.

"Saunders, Mrs Bennett here has just been telling me how her grandson was with her for the whole of yesterday evening. She noticed the money was missing immediately after he went. Isn't that right, Mrs Bennett? You noticed the money had gone after you said goodbye to your grandson, didn't you?" He smiled at her, winningly. "I don't expect it's the first time he's had money from you, is it? I expect you've given him plenty over the years, haven't you?"

"Well, yes I have, of course. But I—"

"—so there you are, Saunders," Terry said. "I think we need to give young master Bennett a visit."

At that, the old lady seemed to come to. She sat up a little straighter, but the hand which was holding her tea trembled more than ever. "Oh, but—"

Terry patted her hand. "—now don't you worry about a thing, Mrs Bennett. DC Saunders and I will sort everything out. You'll get your money back, I guarantee it."

He finished his tea and stood. Clearly, the interview—brief though it was—was at an end. I wanted to ask a whole lot more questions, like, did she see anybody else yesterday? Could the money have gone missing earlier but she didn't notice? Had her grandson ever done anything like this before? Was anything else missing or was it only cash, and was she sure exactly how much cash? Who would know where she kept it? But my sergeant was already halfway out of the room. Shooting the old lady an apologetic glance, I hurried after him.

I didn't know what to do. I was so new and he was the experienced officer, but it seemed to me he'd made his mind up about Gavin Bennett even before he visited the victim, and had then practically coerced Mrs Bennett into agreeing with him.

I sent up a quick arrow prayer, *Please God help me. Tell me what to do.* Quick as a flash, the phrase sprang into my mind, 'Give to Mammon what belongs to Mammon, and to God what belongs to God.' It didn't help. Did this present scenario belong to God or to Mammon? I couldn't decide. Was there something fishy going on, or was it just my inexperience? Was my sergeant merely cutting a few legitimate corners in order to arrive at the correct result more quickly? And if so, did I have the right to challenge him?

I said as casually as I could, "Are we going to consider any other possibilities?"

Terry Anderson stared at me in a pitying way. "When you are a little more experienced, Saunders, you will discover you can discern villains quite easily. You develop a nose for it, in this game. I've met Gavin Bennett before. He's a lout. I picked him up for drug offences over a year ago. You needn't waste any sympathy on him. Ripping off his poor old grandma! That's the sort of bloke you fancy, is it?"

My cheeks burned. That was a cheap shot, but perhaps I asked for it. I hadn't known Gavin Bennett was familiar to him, or that he had a criminal record. I felt really stupid.

"Sorry, Sarge," I mumbled.

He grinned, and his eyes softened. "You know, Saunders, that really suits you, when you flush like that. All that dark hair and those gorgeous brown eyes of yours. They're enough to drive a bloke crazy. And don't worry. You aren't the first rookie to make a mistake and I don't suppose you'll be the last." His voice was kind. "Maybe after this is over, we could go for a drink?"

Was he teasing me? I risked a glance. He was smiling at me, and his blue eyes were warm. As they locked onto mine, I couldn't help but smile in response. He was so nice. I was lucky to have him to show me the ropes. Even so, a drink? What exactly was he expecting out of that? Although I longed to accept, I felt just a tad cautious.

Almost as though he could read my thoughts, he added, "Only a drink, Saunders. It's a tradition in CID. We all go for a drink when the case is closed. I thought you knew that. I wouldn't want you to think I was trying to pick you up, or anything."

Clearly, it was my day for humiliation. I dropped my eyes. Managing a wan smile, I nodded. "That would be good. You think you'll close the case today, then?"

"As near as dammit, if Gavin Bennett is as stupid as I think he is, and is still at home."

Not only was Gavin still at home, he was still in bed, even though it was nearly noon. My opinion of him plummeted.

"Lazy so and so!" Terry muttered, as he hammered on the door.

It was opened a moment or so later by a twenty-something young man clad only in a pair of boxer shorts, and rubbing his eyes. His fair hair was tousled, and he still looked half asleep.

"Going to let us in then, Gavin?" the sergeant said, as he pushed his way past the unprotesting Gavin Bennett.

The front room was a mess, more like a typical teenage room than one belonging to a man in his twenties, with clothes everywhere, books and papers scattered around, an overflowing ashtray, and empty beer cans lying on the table. It didn't have a good feel.

Terry looked around. "Nice place you've got here, Gavin. Glad to see you keep it so tidy."

Gavin Bennett looked mulish. He muttered, "I had a late night, as if it matters to you."

"Oh, it does matter, lad, believe me. We know exactly what you were up to. What was it you bought with the money? Coke? Speed?"

"What money? I don't do drugs, Sergeant. Can't afford it, for one thing. If you must know, I went to see my grandma yesterday evening, and after that I had an essay to write. I'm at college now, and I want to do well."

"Oh, a college boy, is it? Bit old for that, aren't you?" Sarge's voice had taken on a sneering quality which made me feel uncomfortable. But he knew his job. He'd had years of experience cracking criminals, so he knew what he was about. I settled down to listen and learn. He was saying, "I know you students. Snorting stuff up your nose at every opportunity."

Gavin Bennett refused to rise to the bait. He stood stiffly, his arms rigidly by his sides. "I'm a mature student, and I've told you, I don't do that any more. I promised my grandma."

"Ooh! You hear that, Saunders? He promised his grandma! Pity you didn't think about that last night when you nicked her life savings. Where did it all go, Gavin? On the white powder?"

The blood drained from Gavin Bennett's face. He dropped into a chair, his hands to his mouth. "What are you saying? Has my Gran had a break-in? What happened?" Suddenly, he sprang out of the chair. "Is she all right? I must go and see her. She's not hurt, is she? Please tell me she's not hurt."

I intervened, saying in a soothing voice, "No, Gavin, she isn't hurt. A bit shaken up, but other than that, she's fine."

It earned me a glare from Sergeant Anderson, and I was afraid I'd messed up. What was it they'd said at college? Use any and every opportunity to get at the truth. Would we have got at the truth quicker if our suspect believed his grandmother was injured? Heck, this detecting business was more difficult than I'd imagined.

Terry said, "So come on, Gavin. We need you to account for your movements last night. Tell me again, where were you?"

Gavin became quite agitated. He started to pace about the room as he counted off his movements using his fingers. "My last lecture was at 4.15. I called in at the supermarket on the way home, to buy a Chinese. Gran likes a Chinese, so I often get one when I'm going to visit her. Then I went straight round to hers, we ate the Chinese, watched a bit of television, and then I came home. I had a couple of beers, and settled down to my essay. I'm studying economics." He indicated the laptop on the table. "You can have a look, if you like. All the documents are date stamped so you can see exactly when I wrote it. I went to bed about three this morning, and I didn't wake up until you nearly bashed my door down."

Terry didn't appear to listen to any of this. Perhaps that was another cunning tactic. He was prowling around the room taking out books from the bookshelf, poking into cupboards, lifting up cushions. "In that case, you have nothing to hide. You won't mind DC Saunders and me taking a look around, will you?" Before Gavin had a chance to respond, Terry turned to me. "Have you got that, Saunders? The suspect has given us full permission to search his home."

"Hey, hang on a minute. I haven't given you permission for anything!"

"But you wouldn't have any reason for refusing us permission being as you're so clean and white, would you, Gavin?"

Gavin looked defeated. He was neatly trapped, and he knew it. In the end he simply shrugged, and slumped into an armchair. It was all the encouragement Terry needed. Off so fast that I could hardly keep up with him, he explored every room in the little flat, pulling out drawers and tossing clothes on the floor, opening cupboards, searching all the boxes and tins he could find. I followed behind as closely as I could, trying to make notes of his method, but at only five foot four I had little chance of seeing past his six foot two frame.

When we reached the bathroom, he lifted the lid from the cistern and let out a triumphant yell. "Look at this, Saunders! We have him!"

He turned, holding aloft a plastic bag containing a white powder. "Hidden in the loo! I'd have thought he could have found somewhere a little more ingenious to conceal the swag!"

I thought so too. For someone studying the intricacies of economics, it wasn't a very intelligent hiding place.

Gavin Bennett's face was a picture when Terry showed him the plastic bag.

"Is this yours?" Terry asked.

Gavin turned the packet over in his hands. "I've never seen this before in my life. You planted it!"

Terry groaned. "Not that old chestnut," he said, as he carefully placed the evidence into a baggie. "Gavin Anderson, I'm arresting you on suspicion of theft. You don't have to say anything, but whatever you do say will be taken down and may be used in evidence. Do you understand?"

Gavin's face changed from white to red. "You can't do this," he spluttered. "What about my course? I have lectures today and I have to hand in my essay. And I want to see my grandma."

"Ooh, you hear that, Saunders? He wants to see his grandma! You should have thought of that before, lad. Come on, get yourself dressed. We're taking you down to the station. You can protest your innocence down there for as long as you like. We have as long as it takes."

Gavin Bennett turned to me, an agonised expression on his face and an unspoken plea in his eyes. I turned away. There was nothing I could do. I may be naïve, but he wasn't going to catch me that way.

Terry Anderson took me out for a celebratory drink that night. Contrary to what he had said, no one else from the department was there, but to be honest, it was wonderful just being there alone with him outside of work. He was just what I have always dreamed of in a man, caring, solicitous, and lavishing all his attention upon me. He was the best looking man in the bar, too. I lapped it up, thrilled that he had chosen me, despite all my gaffes.

I pushed aside that tiny voice inside my head which kept saying, you know this is a sweetener, don't you? A sweetener so that you won't say anything. What nonsense! The man had done a good day's work and caught a criminal in record time. He was brilliant. Anyway, what could I say, even if I wanted to?

Then Gavin Bennett's frightened and resigned face somehow floated into my consciousness. I tried to push that away, too. There are times when I wish I wasn't a Christian. Somehow I knew that voice would never be silenced until I had done the right thing, whatever the right thing might be. That, I've found, is the penalty of asking God to help.

When he took me home, I resisted inviting Terry in, much as I wanted to. I knew only too well where that might lead, and I didn't want to be any more entangled than I already was. The decision I had to make was difficult enough without any added complications. Terry looked at me with that mocking glance of his, nodded slightly, and drove away—a real gentleman. I had a horrible feeling I'd blown it. He'd never ask me out again.

Please God, I whispered as I knelt by my bed, *let this cup pass from me, but if it really really can't, please tell me what to do and give me the strength to see it through.* Then I picked up my Bible and opened it at random in the New Testament, to see whether God had any particular words for me. It opened at St John's Gospel chapter 6 verse 14, 'Behold, thou art made whole: sin no more, lest a worse thing come unto thee.'

I knew then what I had to do, but I also knew it would mean the end of my career in the police force. There is no way a newbie can act as a whistleblower and expect to survive. Grassing up your fellow officers is the one thing you don't do, especially when that fellow officer is high above you in rank and is extremely popular in the department. I could just see the snide looks, the ostracism, the expressions of disgust. They would probably class me as a rejected female who acted out of jealousy, and I didn't expect Terry Anderson to do me any favours in that department. And for all I knew, Gavin Bennett might well be guilty.

Perhaps I should wait and see what panned out. Perhaps I didn't need to do anything until all the questioning was finished. Perhaps he would be released without charge.

Oh God, I said again, *what should I do?* I opened my Bible once more, hoping it might come up with, 'He will not suffer thy foot to be moved,' from Psalm 121, but it didn't. It opened at the silk bookmark my own grandmother had placed in this old copy of the Bible. On the bookmark was written, 'The Lord will provide.'

In the morning, and in fear and trembling, I went to see the DCI. That alone was enough to raise eyebrows in the department, and Terry glared at me. I poured out my story to the DCI, how I thought it was possible Gavin Bennett had been framed despite his fingerprints on the packet of white powder, and how I thought corners had been cut. The DCI's face grew darker with every sentence I uttered, and I knew I was doomed. I also knew it was unlikely to save Gavin Bennett.

When I'd finished, the DCI said in a cold voice, "And your evidence?"

"Um, well, I don't exactly have any. Not hard evidence, that is, Sir."

"Then I needn't keep you any longer, Constable Saunders. You may go."

Something told me that nothing would happen. So I said the most stupid words I've ever said in my life. I don't know why I said them; they just came out. I said, "Sir, I'm going to the Press."

At that, his eyebrows drew together and his face looked like thunder. He banged his hand on the desk so hard that his papers practically flew off. "Get out," he shouted, in a voice that the whole department must have heard. "And don't come crawling back in here again. We don't employ traitors. You've been here one day, and you think you can come in here accusing a fellow officer, one who has years of experience? One, moreover, who has been put in the position of supervising you and teaching you what you need to know. How dare you? Get out of my sight."

It was the end of my dream. All those years of yearning to be a detective, thrown over for what? My actions wouldn't even form a blip in the grand scheme of things. Nothing I had done would change anything.

Gavin Bennett would still be charged, his grandmother would never see her money again, and would have to suffer the ignominy of a favourite grandson in jail. What a complete and unnecessary waste of time and effort. I'd thrown away my career for nothing.

I railed at God. *That was such a stupid thing to do! And where am I now? With no job, no prospects and absolutely no references. Where on earth do I go from here?*

Then I remembered my grandmother's bookmark, 'The Lord will provide.' It didn't comfort me much, but I kind of clung onto it because I had nowhere else to go.

I found out later that Gavin Bennett was released without charge that day, and that further investigation discovered the cash had been taken by an itinerant worker who had shown up at Mrs Bennett's front door asking to tarmac her drive, and had used her loo. Nearly all her money was returned, and Gavin moved in with her to prevent her making any silly decisions in the future.

Gavin finished his course, passed with honours, and got a good job with a firm of accountants.

How do I know all this? Gavin and I met again three years later, when I eventually landed a job working as a PA in a firm of accountants. God did provide, for I found I loved my new job, especially when I fell in love with and married Gavin Bennett.

Old Mrs Bennett died two years later, but not before we had made her very happy by presenting her with a great-granddaughter. Now the three of us live in Mrs Bennett's dear little cottage, and we're as happy as Larry.

As for Terry Anderson, he never made another grade in the force, remaining a sergeant until he retired. I didn't see him again, but I heard via the grapevine that as he grew older his famous charm began to desert him, and he ended his days a lonely and embittered old man.

'The Lord will provide,' says the Bible. And it's true. But I bet Terry Anderson wishes it wasn't.

23 THE SMALLEST ANGEL

The smallest angel pouted. "It's not fair," she complained. "Why can't I go?"

The bigger angels laughed. "You haven't learned how to fly. How would you get there? You must wait until your wings are strong enough to carry you."

"But the new king will be grown up by then. I want to see the special baby when he's new born and really tiny. I've never seen a baby king before."

"Neither have we," said the bigger angels. "Don't worry, little angel, we'll tell you all about him when we get back. And as a special treat, we'll let you slide down a rainbow into the pot of gold at the bottom. You'll love that."

"Huh!" said the smallest angel, and turned her back.

When the sound of angel wings beating the air and angel voices singing in harmony had faded away, the smallest angel wandered around heaven looking for something to do. She was lonely and bored. Heaven felt empty without the myriads of angels making music and singing and flying.

As she stood on the golden turret of a golden castle wondering whether to jump off just test her wings, she heard a deep voice say, "Be careful, little angel. Be very careful."

Oh dear! God with his deep, kind eyes was watching her. The smallest angel smiled her sweetest, cutest smile, obediently climbed down from the turret and wandered on until she was sure God had turned away. Then, without another thought, she leaped onto a passing cloud and snuggled down into its fluffy depths.

It was so comfortable that in no time at all, the smallest angel had fallen asleep. When she awoke, it was quite dark. The fluffy cloud had drifted far from heaven and was now cold and grey and wet. The smallest angel had no idea where she was. She felt frightened, cold and alone in the dark night sky.

Just then the moon came out, bright and shining with a silvery glow. The smallest angel spotted a moonbeam stretching from the sky towards earth. With the biggest jump ever, she managed to land on the moonbeam, and found herself sliding, sliding, sliding all the way down.

It was a lovely feeling, until the smallest angel saw the tops of mountains rushing towards her. Then she thought it was time to leave so she caught hold of the corner of a passing star. Clinging on for all she was worth, the smallest angel found herself being carried across the night sky by the star.

Looking down she could see men on camels travelling across the desert in exactly the same direction as the star. The star travelled on and on, across plains and forests, seas and towns, with the smallest angel clinging to one of its points. Eventually the smallest angel spotted a village with houses and lights. It felt as though the star was slowing down. Then she heard a sound she knew well, the sound of a heavenly choir.

The smallest angel gulped. She had a feeling she would be in awful trouble. Just at that moment the star suddenly stopped. It stopped over a stable, its light shining into the stable onto a baby snuggled into hay in a manger. But the star stopped so abruptly that the smallest angel shot off. Before she knew what was happening, she fell straight into the manger on top of the baby.

The smallest angel felt like bursting into tears. She feared she might have hurt the baby, and she didn't want to do that. Then the strangest thing happened. The baby opened its eyes, and the smallest angel found herself looking straight into the deep, kind eyes of God.

The smallest angel realised then that God had been watching over her all the time and that God himself was the baby in the manger. With a big smile, the smallest angel hugged the baby tight. The baby put his little hand on her back, and immediately the smallest angel found she could fly.

Happily, she flew off to join all the other angels in the heavenly host. She had found the baby king and that was all she wanted.

24 THE SPIRIT OF LOCH NESS

"…and darkness was upon the face of the deep; and the Spirit of God was moving over the face of the waters…"

The words, dredged from the depths of childhood memories, sprang unbidden into John's mind as he sat at the edge of the loch staring out across the vast expanse of dark water. How did the rest go? He frowned in concentration, but the final remnant of the phrase remained elusive, just out of reach. No matter.

What did anything matter now?

He felt the first black tendrils of despair beginning to curl out across his mind, as the early morning mist curled across the surface of the loch. Where had he gone wrong? It had been so idyllic, a marriage made in heaven. Everyone had said so. They had been a perfect match, he and Jean, full of life and love, delighting in each other's company. What was it Jean used to say with that catchy grin of hers? "John's my best friend as well as my husband."

He grunted. She'd hardly be saying that now! He watched little waves slapping at the shore, and as the silent spirit of the loch began to seep into him, immediately felt little waves of guilt beginning to slap against the edges of his consciousness. So he pushed away the blame by reminding himself firmly that it wasn't all one way. Those terrible, searing words Jean had screamed at him, tears streaming down her face. No wonder he'd slammed out.

Anyway, it was all her fault in the first place. Didn't she realise how much he invested each day in coming home from work to his family, to her and Isabelle, the two people he loved with a bursting intensity which filled his heart and his life? Surely she recognised that such anticipation was the only thing that made work bearable? Wasn't she aware of his need for her, of the suffocating fear which any thought of her absence elicited?

They had shared such heartache over Isabelle, their strange, waif-like daughter, born to be unique, unlike other children. Although neither of them had ever minded about her condition even when it became obvious, and when later on she'd been diagnosed as autistic, it had been hard work from the moment of her birth. But they'd accepted her limitations with equanimity. Where other couples had been forced apart by the demands of such a changeling child, he and Jean had grown closer and closer.

He gazed unseeing across water still dark in the early morning mist, and shivered with cold. Or perhaps with the pain he'd thought locked up forever in the recesses of his memory. He remembered the nights they'd stayed up with Isabelle, taking turns to snatch an hour or two's sleep, while first as a baby then as a toddler she'd been wide awake and vigorously active nearly all night. But they'd worked as a team, he and Jean, prepared to extend their love infinitely to fill their child's needs.

He remembered the hurt of Isabelle's initial inability to respond emotionally to either of them, and the way they'd patiently coaxed and cuddled and played with her. And he remembered the huge joy of that time when she'd fallen and cut her knee and run to Jean to be comforted. How they'd shared that delight! And how miraculously their love for each other had grown and spread and deepened as they'd coped with this extraordinary, oddly gifted daughter.

And now he'd blown it. All those years of self-giving devotion tossed away in one regrettable moment. Goodness knows how Isabelle would react, sitting there so quietly in the shadows at the top of the stairs, little pointed face peering out through the banisters. She'd never heard her parents argue before, let alone rage and physically fight with such venom. Perhaps she would withdraw again into her impenetrable shell, where she sensed safety. Or perhaps she would play the piano for hour after hour after hour, until Jean's brain turned from the pleasure of the music to become scrambled with the repetitive monotony of it all and Jean was stretched taut and tight as cling-film.

John groaned, standing up to flex his muscles and skim a flat pebble over the surface of the loch. It jumped only once, then sank. A bad omen. He shuddered and began to walk, his bones aching with the cold and the mist, or perhaps reflecting the internal ache of his spirit.

How could Jean possibly want a full-time job? It was so unreasonable. Just because Isabelle was at school all day didn't mean she no longer needed her mother at home. Surely Jean could see that? All the dynamics of this family life they'd so carefully built over the years, did they count for nothing? A secure, stable family background was so desperately important for Isabelle. That's what the experts had impressed upon them right from the beginning. And they'd taken it to heart, overwhelmed with their love for their child and the awesome responsibility which had been thrust upon them.

As the first light began to filter through the clouds, the wind increased a little and the surface of the loch became quite choppy. Almost as though he was resonating with the changes in the loch, panic started to rise within him. He couldn't believe the violence of his anger, now spent. He, normally so calm, so placid; a rock on which Jean could fasten, where she could rest secure. But a rock which had become suddenly sword-sharp and dangerous, which hadn't protected Jean but had damaged her. How could he have done that? Was he mad, a potential psychopath with no control?

He couldn't bear to picture her face, yet it stubbornly appropriated his mind with its blood seeping from her nose and that eye already beginning to swell and close. He stifled a sob as he fearfully contemplated the hidden monster within him.

A movement on the loch caught his eye. He strained to see through the dark grey of early dawn and the swirls of mist. Surely not the Loch Ness monster! Even in his disturbed and fragile state John refused to believe in that. No, it was something much more ethereal, something slight and delicate. He moved carefully towards the movement, his vision growing as dawn expanded.

Soon he could make out a sprite, an elfin figure dancing on the dancing waves, so that he was unsure which was creature and which was water. He paused spellbound, as the fairy creature wove enchanted patterns of movement, turning, pirouetting, darting motion. She was absorbed in her dance, at one with the waves on which she was poised.

Unaccountably, as the sun stole tentatively above the horizon, John felt his mood begin to lighten. Perhaps the spirit of Loch Ness wasn't dark depths of despair in rising terror, but was this bewitching water-nymph who could dance on the surface of the loch. He inched closer, creeping slowly, cautiously, anxious not to frighten or disturb, focusing intently on the whirling Spirit, white-blonde hair wind-blown from her pixie face. But she spotted him.

"Don't stop," he pleaded. "It was so beautiful."

She nodded solemnly. "I've finished." And she turned and ran back along the landing stage now emerging from the mist.

"I thought you were dancing on the water," John confided.

Her eyes lit up and she smiled a secret, elfin smile, but she didn't answer. He added, "What are you doing out here alone?"

"Dancing. But I'm going now. Come." And she beckoned John as she slipped into the undergrowth along hidden paths hitherto unnoticed by him.

John was reminded of the sirens of old who would lure unsuspecting males to their doom. Yet he followed, unable to resist, captivated by the ephemeral charm of this Spirit of Loch Ness. What did she want with him? Was the hope licking at the corners of his mind all an illusion, an elevation designed only to plunge him finally and irrevocably into black, black depths?

She led him away from the loch shore, through fern and bracken, thorn and thicket, until he was disorientated, uncertain of the direction in which they were travelling. And she moved lightly, quickly, confidently, never pausing in consideration of his clumsiness. He felt like a mammoth crashing through the underbrush in the wake of a wispy moth.

He regained his bearings as they emerged through a clearing onto the winding lane which led down to the shore from the cottage. John's heart began to thud breathlessly as they neared the cottage door, but Isabelle seemed oblivious of any difficulty as she scampered on. Perhaps she had already forgotten he was following her.

John stopped, his euphoria suddenly evaporating. His daughter was after all no Spirit, merely a slightly damaged human being. How foolish to imagine for one fleeting instant that she might be a portent, a symbol of hope.

Her dance had activated the security device over the door as they approached, so that the front garden was instantly flooded with light. The front door opened and Jean stood framed in the doorway.

As John tremulously looked at her, fear so huge that it threatened to overflow his mind, he saw her arms open towards him. He stumbled towards her, and clutched her to him. They clung to each other, the love of years so much stronger than the fury of one moment.

Out of the corner of his eye John noticed the child slip off unconcerned towards the swing. And that long-forgotten phrase leaped into his mind:

"….And God said, Let there be light! And there was light."

25 TRAVELLING RIGHT

"Mum, can Wanda come and play after school tomorrow?"

Beth smiled indulgently as her daughter finished scraping the bowl, leaving a layer of cake mixture all round her mouth. "Who's Wanda? Haven't heard of her before."

"She's a new girl in my class. Nobody likes her, except me. I played with her at dinner time. She's really nice. But all the others tease her. Some of them bully her, so she needs me there. Anyway, I really like her."

"Oh Abi! You and your waifs and strays! Maybe we should stick a sign on the front gate saying, 'Abigail's home. All lonely people or broken animals stop here.' What do you think? Look, do we really have to have her? Dad and I are going to that village meeting tomorrow evening, remember. We're dropping you off at Grandma's on the way."

"Pleeeze Mum! She could come for a couple of hours and we could sample the cakes together. You know you like it when my friends eat your cakes. And Wanda's not like that hedgehog I found, nor the baby rabbit with mixy."

"Or the owl with the broken wing?"

But Beth was grinning. In truth she was delighted that her daughter was showing strong indications of compassion at such a young age and was keen to encourage her.

"Look, Abi. I'll have to speak to Wanda's mum, to make sure it's alright with her. Can you find out her phone number for me? I'll ring and a have a chat with her."

"Thanks, Mum. You're brilliant." And Abigail flung triumphant arms around her mother, blissfully unaware of the stickiness of her fingers on Beth's shirt. Beth laughed, gently disentangling herself.

"Come on, kiddo. Washing up time. Let's get those hands into some soapy water. You wash, I'll dry."

Rose Washburn sounded nice on the phone, although Beth had a little difficulty understanding her unfamiliar soft, Irish burr. There weren't many Irish in this tiny, South Norfolk village where most families had lived for generations, so it was a good thing, Beth reflected, to enrich the indigenous population.

Not that she herself had been born in Kirkby Thorpe. She and Brian were incomers who had moved from Norwich some five years ago, when Abigail was just three. Abigail had been an answer to prayer after ten childless years of marriage, but at least they had been able to save during those ten years, enabling them to buy one of the new, detached houses on the outskirts of the village.

It had been a bit tricky at first. Some of the village youngsters were unable to afford any property in the village and had been forced to move to the city, triggering resentment against the newcomers. But Brian and Beth were friendly and outgoing, attended the local church and joined in all village activities. And a year later when Abigail had started at the village school, all antipathy had finally vanished. Now, Beth felt, they really were accepted as part of the village.

Remembering her own loneliness during her early days in the village, Beth invited Rose to drop in for coffee one day. Rose sounded surprisingly grateful for the invitation, a gratitude which was repeated when Beth offered to pick the girls up after school next day and bring Wanda home for tea. She also offered to drop Wanda back in the early evening, but Rose refused, saying that she could easily collect her daughter at six o'clock. As Beth replaced the phone she found herself looking forward to meeting Rose Washburn.

Wanda was a pretty little thing, slighter than the more robust Abigail and as dark as Abigail was fair. Both girls wore their hair long and both had changed into jeans and T-shirts after school. They were engrossed in a game involving books, sophisticated dolls and water, which Beth had laughingly insisted took place on the patio rather than in the lounge.

Beth had been struck by Wanda's rather old-fashioned politeness, always addressing her as 'Mrs Kitchener' and remembering to say 'please' and 'thank you'. It was a welcome change from most of Abigail's school friends, who tended to be informal to the point of casualness, generally addressing Beth by her Christian name. The two girls played well together and were no trouble. Beth was always pleased to receive Abigail's playmates, believing that children without siblings needed plenty of friends around them. And there was something about Wanda which appealed to Beth. She seemed quieter than Abigail's other friends and a little timid. As they had a school library book with them which Abigail was reading aloud to Wanda during the game, Beth wondered whether perhaps she was a slow learner with special needs. Beth made very sure to be especially gentle and welcoming.

Rose called for her daughter at exactly six o'clock. About ten years younger than Beth, she was very like her daughter with long black hair hanging nearly to her waist but tied back into a pony tail, which made her look even younger. Like Wanda, she was slight of build with her tiny figure encased in jeans, topped by a colourful shirt.

Beth liked her immediately. "You must be Rose! Do come in and see the girls at play, they really seem to have taken to each other. You have a lovely daughter, Rose. You must be so proud of her."

Rose smiled shyly and followed her hostess. When Wanda spotted her, she ran to her mother's side, but Abigail protested.

"Oh Mum! Does she have to go already? Can't we have another ten minutes? It's so early."

"Now come on, Abi! You know what we agreed. And we don't want to keep Wanda's Mummy waiting. Wanda can come again another day."

Abigail pouted. "It's not fair! Just because you have a silly meeting - "

"Abigail!" her mother said sharply, suddenly ashamed of her daughter beside her beautifully behaved friend.

Rose said pacifically, "We have to go. But perhaps you would like to come and play with Wanda one day?" and Beth smiled gratefully at her as Abigail immediately perked up and resorted to her usual sunny self.

"You will come for coffee now you know where we live, won't you?" Beth urged Rose, as mother and daughter made their way to the car. "I can introduce you to the village and tell you all about the various village activities. I'm sure you'll be happy here."

"Thank you, I'd like that. And thank you for looking after Wanda. She doesn't have many friends. I'm glad she's met your daughter. You're very kind."

Since it was impossible to hurry Grandma under any circumstances, Beth and Brian were late for their meeting, squeezing into the back of the village hall just as proceedings started. Inevitably, the village hall was packed. Any issue to do with Travellers, as the politically correct District Council insisted on referring to the gypsies, raised strong passions. And Travellers illegally encamped on David and Jocelyn Raiment's set-aside field, close to the village street, resulted in predictable fury.

The Raiments were well liked in Kirkby Thorpe. Beth and Brian had become firm friends with them over the years through church, where David was churchwarden and Brian treasurer. Beth and Jocelyn were both in the Mothers' Union and often met for fund raising events, some of which were held in the Raiment's sixteenth century farmhouse or on the farm. The set aside field was an especial bonus for the church. It was perfectly placed for the church fete and the strawberry teas, both of which had been written into the calendar since last year. So there was real disgruntlement amongst the church population over the illegal gypsy encampment.

The Parish Council Chairman introduced the platform party; two representatives from the District Council, two representatives from the police force and five Parish Councillors, all looking suitably serious. The Travellers had not been invited.

After a short introduction by the chairman, it was free for all. Emotion immediately began to rise.

A short, dark man with a bull neck and shaven head revealing a tattoo of a serpent on his neck, shot to his feet before anyone else had a chance to think. He waved his fist belligerently. "What's the police doin', I'd like to know? These people, they're no better than animals. They're filthy leeches, that what they are. Living off the backs of decent people."

He sat down to loud cries of, "Hear, hear."

"Thank you, Mr Braden," the Chairman hastily intervened. "I think we all need to use temperate language when discussing this issue. Nothing is to be gained by emotive remarks without any foundation - "

" - you calling me a liar?" Benny Braden was back on his feet, his face a mottled red. "There's houses been burgled and stuff nicked from sheds since them gyppos come. We all know who's responsible. So what's the police doin' about it? 'Cos if they don't do nothing, we will!"

There was a rumble of agreement in the hall.

The Chairman said, "Please be careful, Mr Braden. I would not like to have you arrested because of racist remarks. We can at least show common courtesy to the Travellers. Perhaps we should invite Mr and Mrs Raiment to speak. The Travellers are camped on their land. And please remember, ladies and gentlemen, we can only deal with facts, not gossip or innuendo. Unless you have hard facts backing your case, there is nothing we can do."

"Nothing?" Another, older man had stood. Beth recognised him as Henry Whitehouse, Head Teacher of the village Church of England Primary school which Abigail attended. "Illegal encampments pose a real problem for Traveller children. The Travellers are moved on from pillar to post, so these children never get a settled education. And it costs huge resources from our school budget to set up adequate support for the children as we are obliged by law to do, only to find that they move on in a week or so. Something must be done for the sake of the children and our school."

A well-spoken woman clad in designer clothing chimed in, "Surely the police have a duty to keep the law? This encampment is illegal. What's more, the Travellers pay no council tax, yet as we've just heard, they use public facilities like the rest of us. And after they leave, who foots the clean-up bill? I hear it's usually massive."

David Raiment stood up. Beth strained to hear, but the room fell quiet as he began to speak in measured tones.

"I'm afraid we - Jocelyn and myself - pick up the bill and it may run into thousands. Because the Travellers are on private land, the owner of the land is responsible for all expenses. Nothing falls to the tax payer or the council. Naturally we have been down to the site and politely asked the Travellers to move on, but as yet they show no signs of doing so. These people don't understand common courtesy. Our next action is to use bailiffs, but I hope it won't come to that. Not only would that cost even more, but it might provoke violence. No, we would like this meeting to support us by calling on the District Council, the Parish Council and the police service to work together and use some muscle here. Why should it all be left to us? We didn't invite the Travellers. It's not fair."

Beth felt herself growing hot with indignation. David was right. It was so unfair. These people were there illegally, were known to leave filth behind, paid nothing towards public services and coincidentally the crime rate, usually zero in Kirkby Thorpe, had already risen. She glanced at Brian, who was nodding vigorously at David's words, his colour rising and a small vein in his temple throbbing. He was getting worked up, as was the whole room.

"Let's go get them ourselves!" somebody yelled, to loud choruses of agreement.

The police sergeant stood. "I must remind you that any illegal action on your part will result in arrests. Please leave this to the council and the police. I can assure you that we have your best interests at heart."

"Oh yeah?" jeered a voice from the crowd. "Since when? Only interests you have are them gyppos, Irish scum! Bend over backwards for them, but don't never uphold the law for us."

The mood of the crowd was growing ugly, with groups of men and women apparently quite prepared to attack the Travellers' camp. Benny Braden produced a baseball bat seemingly from nowhere, and as if on signal, several more baseball bats and wooden sticks suddenly appeared. Beth realised that it had been set up beforehand, with the meeting just an excuse to wind people up, rallying support and an excuse for violence. She was conscious of fear at the pit of her belly.

Then all at once she made a connection. She didn't know quite what triggered it, but she suddenly realised who Abigail's new friend was. No wonder none of the other children would play with Wanda. Beth's mind flipped to Rose Washburn, who had seemed so nice. But that long, black hair and that Irish accent! Clearly she was a gypsy.

Beth felt sick. She liked the woman and her child. She had invited them into her home. And now they could be in real danger from angry villagers. But there was nothing she could do. She, Beth, could hardly stand up against the whole village, and David and Jossy were her good friends. She was only at the meeting to support them. Anyway, what would Brian think? She didn't want divorce in her family, thank you very much. Besides, the camp was illegal. There was no getting away from that fact. The Chairman had said they must deal in facts. Well, that was one. How could Beth in good conscience support anything illegal? Obviously she couldn't, unless she wanted to throw away everything she and Brian had worked so hard to achieve in Kirkby Thorpe. And she had to think of Abigail. Kids can be cruel and some of those parents would make very sure that their children gave Abigail a vicious time if her mother stepped out of line. No, she'd best sit quiet and do nothing. After all, she didn't have to join in with village hassle and she would never concur with violence. And if she did nothing, she couldn't be held responsible. Could she?

Even as these thoughts raced through her mind, Beth knew that she was trying to convince herself. She also knew just what she stood to lose; five years of hard work in the village and some good friends, to say nothing of her own marriage. Beth gulped, fear filling her heart.

But almost without thinking, she found herself on her feet. She stood on a chair to be seen above the crowd. She saw Jocelyn watching her expectantly and knew regretfully that Jossy's face would soon change. She heard herself say, "Now listen! If we go down there with baseball bats, it's us who'll be the animals. Please. Let's think about this rationally. The Travellers are people. They're families like us with children and grandchildren and they deserve a bit of compassion. How would any of you like to be hounded out, constantly pushed on by hostile villages? I know they're parked illegally and that can't be right, but isn't there somewhere in the village where we could help make a proper site for them? After all, if they had a site which was properly managed, perhaps there wouldn't be so much mess. What are they supposed to do with their rubbish without bins? Can't we help them instead of hurting them?"

Then, as someone jeered, "She's gone mad!" and someone else cried, "Traitor!" reaction set in and Beth's legs began to tremble. What had she done? They'd have to leave Kirkby Thorpe for sure. But to her astonishment, she felt Brian climb onto a chair beside her and grab for her hand. "It's a free country and we all have free speech. You may not agree with my wife, but I'm proud of her. She had the courage to stand up and be counted. And I have a suggestion. What about the old Maltings? It's been empty for years, it's rat infested, it's an eye-sore and no-one can be found to buy it. How about the District Council putting its money where its mouth is and helping the Travellers to buy it? And if we're really a Christian village, maybe some of us could help to clear it out and make it fit for human habitation."

The crowd howled. They were so angry that Beth was afraid she and Brian might be lynched. She wasn't quite sure how they stumbled out of the meeting, to the background of jeers and catcalls and with Jocelyn's stricken face etched on her mind. She knew the next few weeks and months and probably years would be painfully hard, but although she was still afraid, that no longer mattered. She knew she had done the right thing and Brian had stood with her. Nothing else mattered.

"No wonder our daughter's the way she is, looking after waifs and strays," she reflected in the car on the way home. "Look at her parents! Always taking on lost causes and losing popularity to boot. But doesn't it feel good inside?"

Beside her, Brian nodded. "We may not be able to do much and we certainly won't get any thanks, but we'll help the Travellers as best we can, you and I together against the world."

Beth thought, 'I may have lost some friends, but I'm pretty sure I'll have made at least one new one.'

And she looked forward to getting to know Rose Washburn.

ABOUT THE AUTHOR

Janice B. Scott was born in Rugby, Warwickshire, but the family moved to Croydon before she was two years old.

Janice attended the local Infants' and Primary schools, winning a scholarship at the age of ten to Croydon High School, a Direct Grant School for girls, and a member of the Girls' Public Day School Trust.

On leaving school she won a place at King's College Hospital in Dulwich to study physiotherapy, emerging as a Chartered Physiotherapist and working in the National Health Service for two years, prior to training at The Middlesex Hospital in London as a teacher of physiotherapy.

During this time she met and married Ian, also a Chartered Physiotherapist and teacher of physiotherapy.

The couple taught physiotherapy at The London Hospital for three years, during which their first two children—Fiona and Alexander—were born, before the family moved to Fakenham in Norfolk where Janice and Ian set up in private practice. Seven years later their third child—Rebecca—was born. Janice and Ian were in practice in Fakenham for a total of twenty two years.

In the late eighties Janice experienced a call to ordained ministry. She trained with the East Anglian Ministerial Training Course, qualifying in 1992, before women could be ordained priest in England. She served two years as a deacon in Fakenham before being ordained priest with the first group of women at Norwich Cathedral in 1994.

In 1995 the family moved to Eaton in Norwich, where Janice became stipendiary curate at St. Andrew's and Christchurch.

In 1999 she felt a call to the post of rector at Dickleburgh And The Pulhams, six rural parishes in South Norfolk, where the family spent ten happy years. During this time Janice was appointed Rural Dean of Redenhall Deanery, Honorary Canon of Norwich Cathedral, and completed an MA in pastoral theology.

Janice's writing career started when she won a radio short story competition, followed by having a short story accepted for Angus Wilson's 'Writers Of East Anglia'. She was a regular contributor to 'Pause For Thought' on Radio Norfolk until the programme was axed, and is a staff writer for Redemptorist Publications.

Her internationally renowned website, 'Sermons And Stories' was taken over by CSS Publishing Co., a Christian publishing company in the USA, where she writes as 'The Village Shepherd'. CSS have published the first two volumes of 'Children's Stories From The Village Shepherd', and the third volume is in the pipeline.

Aware of the gulf between church attenders and the non-church attending public, Janice decided to write a trilogy of novels featuring Rev. Polly Hewitt, a warm, human and fun-loving priest whose Christianity is practical and down-to-earth. The third novel in the series, 'Vengeance Lies In Wait', is a murder mystery, but due to demand, the series continues! The fourth novel is due out in 2013 and is again a murder mystery. The novels all open up some of the deeper questions of life which every human being faces, in a non-threatening and easy manner which can be enjoyed by those of faith or those with no faith at all.

Janice also enjoys writing just for fun, and if you have reached thus far in this slim volume, you will have realised that few of the stories in this anthology have any deeper meaning. They are simply to be enjoyed.

Janice B. Scott's website is www.janice-scott.com

Made in the USA
Charleston, SC
06 August 2012